Mountains and Meditations
A Quabbin Quills Anthology

Perpetual Imagination
Boston • Northampton • New York

881 Main St #10
Fitchburg, MA 01420

info@perpetualimagination.com

ISBN: 978-0-578-50098-0

Library of Congress Control Number in process for this title.

The Hills Glow

The hills glow an old autumn yellow
The wind craves the night
A generator's hum
The suncitymountains
The treerivervalleys
The trailfeetmud
Everything is coagulating
Merging to the center
Oneness
Hills spread wide
Sharp spikes and domes
We call the mountains, "HOME".

Ned Green October 7, 1997

From Cutting A Bond with the Long Trail, Ned Green's Long Trail journals as compiled by his "ole ma" Clare Green, pages 31-32. Ned, age 26, died in 2001 due to an ice climbing accident. He worked passionately in all of the New England Mountain Clubs while journaling extensively. This poem is an excerpt from the book which is also a fundraiser for the Green Mountain Club and for a scholarship given each year to a deserving graduating senior at Pioneer Valley Regional School. The book is available at local libraries or online at GMC.

CONTENTS

BEYOND THE CLOUDS   1
Michael Young

OUR POND   4
Jan VanVaerenewyck

THE VIEW FROM THE TOP   5
Sue Buck

LATE DAY AT THE GAZEBO   9
Kay Deans

OUR NEIGHBOR   10
Clare Green

IN HOPE   13
Karyl J. Leslie

A SKUNK AT THE COUNTY FAIR   14
Dennis F. King

MAGICAL CREATURES   18
Steven Michaels

A CAT BY ANY OTHER NAME   20
Sharon A Harmon

A THREE-DOG LIFE   22
Diane Kane

THE LURE   24
Michael Young

LADY, GO FIND THE GOATS!   25
Kay Deans

OUT IN THE WOODS   31
   Karyl J. Leslie

NOW HEAR THIS   32
   Kathy Chencharik

BENEATH MY FEET   34
   Liz Day

TOGETHER WE BUILD   35
   Sonya Shaw Wirtanen

CUTTING A BOND WITH THE LONG TRAIL *Selections* 39
   Entries & Poems by Ned Green

FOR THE GREATER GOOD   40
   Nancy Tatro

THE LOST TOWNS OF QUABBIN   42
   Nancy Damon Burke

MARIGOLD VERONA MEETS MADAME PELE   45
   Linda J. Donaldson

SPIRITUS MUNDI   49
   Steven Michaels

HUBRIS   51
   James Thibeault

NIGHT   60
   Jon Bishop

INVISIBLE HITCHHIKER   61
   Clare Green

STAN LEE, SOUTHWEST, AND SHAKESPEARE   63
   Steven Michaels

PRIESTLY FRIENDS   65
   Mary Louise Owen

SEASONS   70
Nancy Damon Burke

THE FOG HAS RISEN   72
Joanne McIntosh-Davidson

A RETRO TALE   75
Sally Sennott

CHIRPING   87
Steven Michaels

PROFILES   88
James Thibeault

LAST EXIT BEFORE THE TOLL   95
Steven Michaels

THE TEN-FOOT-TALL MAN   101
Dennis F. King

ODE TO JANET GUTHRIE   107
Steven Michaels

SUNDAY AT GRANDPA'S   108
Diane Kane

THE ROAD, THE RIVER, AND THE HAIRPIN TURN   110
Dennis F. King

LAWN CARE   113
Steven Michaels

JOURNEY FROM THE VALLEY OF DEATH TO THE
MOUNTAIN OF HOPE   115
Mary Louise Owen

SOFT AWAKENING   118
Nancy Damon Burke

MORE LOVE   119
 Clare Green

ECHOES OF MY SOUL   126
 Sonya Shaw Wirtanen

BEYOND THE FARAWAY ROOM   129
 Mary Louise Owen

TENTATIVE BRAVERY   131
 Linda J. Donaldson

VISUAL LINES   132
 Steven Michaels

THE CONFIDANTE   133
 Maggie Scarf

FLOWERS FOR THE DEVIL   135
 Dennis F. King

THE WHITCOMB INN   136
 Nancy Damon Burke

A SIMPLE PRAYER   143
 Karyl J. Leslie

MORNING GLORY INCIDENT   144
 Linda Donaldson

FIRST LOVE   147
 Mary Louise Owen

OUR CONTRIBUTORS   155
 QUABBIN QUILLS Production Team   155
 ABOUT OUR AUTHORS   157

BEYOND THE CLOUDS

Michael Young

My quest began with a journey from East Orange, NJ, to the Cathedral of St. John the Divine in New York City. At the cathedral, I learned a moving meditation – Dances of Universal Peace or Sufi Dancing. I was going through a transformation in my personal, professional and faith life. Not only was I dancing in church, which was unheard of in my Presbyterian background, but I was chanting foreign phrases and names of God. Wanting to learn more, I went to a Sufi Camp in Woodstock, NY. My heart blasted wide open from spiritual practices and I fell in love with a woman. My spiritual teacher wisely suggested that we test our relationship by going to a camp in Chamonix, France across from Mt. Blanc. The relationship did not stand the test, but it got us to the camp. When I saw the blissful state of campers coming down from the mountain, I was propelled to go on a five-day silent retreat.

It's a long way from the suburbs of New Jersey to the French Alps, where I did my retreat in a cave above the treeline, which I discovered for the occasion. My favorite memory of the Alps was when I completed my meditation and stepped outside one evening. The sun had just set and the world had disappeared beneath a multicolored blanket of clouds. All that remained visible were the tops of the mountains, projecting through the clouds. I was literally sitting on top of the world.

The journey from there to the North Quabbin took me through the Catskill Mountains and the Berkshires. While I lived in a cabin in the Catskills, I watched trees saying their evening prayers, bending toward the setting sun. A short distance from my cabin was a waterfall that played its song into my consciousness. When I found moments where I was unaware of the waterfall's song, I would bring my wandering mind back to the waterfall.

In the Berkshires, I went on several retreats at the Abode of the Message, a Sufi community created in a historic Shaker Village. There was a strong desire to do everything with consciousness, whether in meditation or everyday life. That included planting the community garden, building single-family houses, or renovating Shaker buildings. There was a gentle stream tumbled and gurgled past the retreat huts. My young daughter declared that fairies lived in that enchanted glen. A school for the grade-school children was housed in one of the buildings. There was a constant presence of playful children in the courtyard or the playground. Their innocence and their joy pervaded the atmosphere and gentled the adults. A teepee housed a nature center based on Native American wisdom and lore. The mysticism of East and West was consciously connected.

There is plenty of nature in the North Quabbin to inspire my meditation. It could be while fishing the Millers River or sitting on the quiet shore of Tully Lake. Waterfalls play their tune at Doanes Falls or Royalston Falls. Above all, in the distance rises Mt. Monadnock. Our log house sits well back from the far treeline before us. The seasonal procession of the sun goes from far left in summer, over near the farmhouse on the hill, to far right during winter, behind the ancient oaks that line our road. As I sit on my front porch, sipping my morning coffee, facing east and the rising sun, I sense the space before me – the expanse of yard and hayfield.

I feel the roundness of the earth and the secure pull of gravity. Evenings, I watch the setting sun as it slides behind the western trees. The forest beyond creates a fortress wall that shields us from the rest of the world.

While summer is time to expand and be aware of outside, winter is time to go inside, figuratively and literally. My morning meditation moves to where it is warm. As I kindle the fire in the wood stove, I sing my thanks and pray for health. Being aware of the sun's journey is replaced by gazing at the fire through the smoky stove glass. The energy of the new day's tasks and promises is mirrored in the promise of the kindling fire.

When I was still living in New Jersey, a friend invited me to present my slideshow meditation, 'Peace Flows from Within," as the sermon for her Sunday church service. To a musical soundtrack, images of candles, flowers, mountains and sunsets faded into one another. After the service, one of the parishioners, a South Jersey farmer, came up to talk to me.

He remarked, "You know, sometimes when I get done with my chores, I go lean on the fence and watch the sun go down. Other times, when I'm tired or the weather is bad, I just rest in my recliner and watch the fire…" Then in puzzled amazement, he asked, "You mean I'm meditatin'?"

We may not have Alpine peaks poking through clouds in the North Quabbin, but we do have streams & waterfalls, fields and forests, sunrise and sunsets and scenes of vastness and beauty worthy of meditation and inspiration.

Yes, I mean I'm meditatin'.

OUR POND

Jan VanVaerenewyck

I linger in the fading sun

my list of chores still undone.

The pair of ducks I'm watching here

swim in silence, nothing to fear.

The birches are white against the sky

and here, no there, small birds fly.

I'm anxious as I mark the time,

my thoughts removed from the sublime.

But still I watch the loveducks dance,

envious of their spring romance.

THE VIEW FROM THE TOP

Sue Buck

It had taken half of our life, but we finally arrived at the top of the hill. Some of us wondered just who got to decide when we would be going "over the hill." We marveled that we had all made it to the top, never mind going over it. No matter; we were there. Our little entourage had been largely unnoticed the whole time. Being invisible was how we liked it. At least, we thought we did. Maybe we just said that because it was what we'd always known. Nobody fussed about what they had to carry or where they belonged in line. We all knew our place and we knew what we were responsible for.

I can't say it was a smooth climb. I also can't report that no one was hurt. I suppose we were all injured at some point or another, but none of us were completely broken. Sometimes we were careless and got in way over our heads. Sometimes others were careless with us. We might sense a dangerous situation, but we were ill prepared to handle it. We lacked the necessary tools. It was just that simple. Our injuries did not define us or stop us. I think we managed quite well. We knew to laugh and dance when the coast was clear. We held our faces toward the sun when it shone. We never lost the ability to find the smallest glimmer of light, even in the middle of very dark times.

As we approached the top, it suddenly became quiet. We needed to take a minute, both separately and collectively. This accomplishment deserved recognition and respect. We hadn't merely conquered this hill. We had decided to survive. So we sat. At the top of the hill. We exchanged tiny, almost non-discernable nods amongst us. We were not prideful. We were certainly not showy. We were relieved. I turned around for a brief moment and nearly lost my balance.

"Don't look back!" they all shouted. "If you look back, you will second guess every step we just took. We will lose perspective and momentum. Looking back will only hurt us all." I followed their advice and turned away from where we'd come.

"Can I look out?" I asked. They replied in unison, nearly achieving harmony.

"Yes!"

So I opened my eyes and looked out for myself.

The view before me was beautiful; nearly limitless. I'd never imagined the future as being limitless before. I felt I might be getting a little ahead of myself being more excited than afraid for the first time. I made the decision to stay with excitement and told fear to go sit in the shade...take a load off. I suggested we all might benefit from unpacking a bit. We didn't need to take out all of what we had brought, just the things that could meet our basic needs in the moment.

Mercy and grace sprang into action. It was their nature to prepare any place we rested. They had a particular knack for making us all feel welcome; no matter where we were at the time. Without fail, they leveled the ground we all stood on so we could sense the solid foundation beneath us. My heart opened a jar of water. It was all she needed to beat again with joy and fresh purpose. She passed it to my mind, who was licking her lips in anticipation of the same relief my heart was feeling. My mind had struggled more than any of us during the climb. Reality and dreams had, as usual, sat across from each other and were having a staring contest. I bravely suggested they try sitting next to each other, facing the same direction. It might be an asset to them both. They readjusted their positions and sacrificially cleaned off each other's glasses. They had not decided whose view was more accurate, but they agreed they both deserved the chance to see clearly.

Joy took the rocks out of anger's backpack and extolled the virtues of travelling light. Forgiveness kept trying to tighten her boot straps. She often struggled with this adjustment, but she was learning. Sadness and bitterness sat alone, away from the rest of us. They still tagged along even when they sensed that the rest of us wished they weren't there. We were not especially fond of them, but they had always been a part of us as long as we could remember. They were just as legitimate as anyone else there...for better or for worse. We all knew that they slowed us down, but until they found a place on the path to really be at peace and rest, we would never pretend that they were not a part of us.

Hope finally came and sat next to me. She had stayed in the back for some time now. I had often invited her to join us, but at the same time, I was reluctant to acknowledge her existence. I could never look her in the face. I had never trusted her. Hope always threw me off. She made me feel disoriented and vulnerable. This time, I did not turn away from her. I was afraid that such a risky maneuver would cost me what measure of balance I had found. I knew I needed her. Slowly, she reached her arm around and moved right into me. She began to nudge debris off my shoulders as I put my head in my hands and sobbed.

"I am so exhausted. Now that I know that I really want to be here, I don't think I can do this." She sweetly suggested I delegate a bit to lighten my burden and become more whole. I thought about it, but fear had stood up and reminded me how that had gone before. Everything I had trusted to my heart had been lost. My mind was easily distracted and often felt splintered.

Hope took my face in her hands and helped me see more clearly.

"All hearts suffer loss. It's part of the equation of loving. Minds have ways of protecting themselves...like porcupines. Sometimes, they need to push back. It's survival...not failure. All of you have recovered. None of you are crippled. If you continue to behave like you are, I will never be able to take the lead."

I knew she was right. We all did. I stepped back a bit to give hope some room. One by one, everyone came near to her. Even sadness and bitterness embraced her; I think they wanted to make sure she was real...see what she felt like. We all had questions for her. Hope did not have all the answers, but she had a perspective and confidence that we had never experienced on our own. Hope would change how we moved forward. It was not immediately clear to any of us how much of our baggage we would still be carrying. There was time to figure this out. It was enough, at that moment, just to believe that the rest of our journey could be different. We stepped back together and let hope take the lead. We weren't quite over the hill yet, but we all agreed on one thing...we loved the view from the top.

LATE DAY AT THE GAZEBO

Kay Deans

The sun lifts my spirits.
Gentle noises of the garden
and a visiting breeze
join me.
They are welcome.

I sit facing the sun.
A slight breath of air
cools the back of my neck.
A plane overhead,
a thump below,
and indistinct sounds of a boombox…
The dogs have found shelter in the shade
under leaves that dance in the wind.

My mind relaxes,
my thoughts coalesce.
My pen glides across the page,
stopping only
while my thoughts catch up.

Shadows grow longer.
The air turns cooler.
A steady hum of traffic
marks the end of the workday.
Time now to eat,
relax,
and sleep.

OUR NEIGHBOR

Clare Green

"Please take this meatloaf dinner to Brenda. I think she'll enjoy it," said Mom.

"Sure will!" I replied.

I loved walking the brief wooded path to her cozy cottage of a home. My feet trod the simple, safe trail to her doorstep. A functional bird bath decorated her small front yard. Bird feeders hung from her kitchen windows. Squirrels scurried to forage dropped seeds. She loved to observe nature's many changes. I knocked on the door and politely waited, as I had been told to do.

"Come in, Clare. Thank you! Can you sit for a moment and visit?"

"OK."

The memory of that inviting comfy chair by the door adjacent to the grand piano was perfect for my small body to sink into and feel at home. Brenda asked questions about school and family. It felt luxurious to share a conversation with her. Back home, I was often told to "quiet-down" by my siblings, being the youngest of five children. Before the visit ended I asked, "Brenda, would you please measure me again to see if I have grown taller?"

"I'd be delighted. Let's go to the kitchen wall."

There on the wall were all the neighborhood kids' names and heights. "Half an inch taller. Yes!" Brenda marked it in pencil and wrote the date in her classic, cryptic handwriting. Even my large baby doll was measured and her name was placed on the wall, "Baby Doll." She was about as tall as the dogs that were measured.

"Bye, Brenda, thanks for the visit and have a nice dinner." In a minute's time, I ran the path home, now that my arms were free from holding the warm meal.

A favorite pastime of Brenda's was taking long walks in the woods with Shadow, our family collie. Through the fields of brightly colored phlox she stood barely a foot above Shadow. No matter my age, Brenda was always the same to me - kind, interesting and elderly.

Her dark-shingled cabin with a very spacious art room was nestled in the woods behind our family homestead in Wilton, Connecticut. Classical tunes often lulled us to sleep during the summer months when Brenda played her grand piano. Our family was pleased to have Brenda for a neighbor for many years.

It was a sweet time to grow up - the 1950's. Neighbors along the road became gentle extensions of family life. There was a respectful art to visiting, conversing and nibbling assorted offerings. Sharing time with a neighbor was considered very special, and we were told never to stay too long. Don't overstay your welcome. Be polite. Time stood still and enfolded us in its graciousness. Neighborly visits were like simple gifts which resonated in our hearts. Those assorted visits taught us to listen, practice manners, relax and appreciate differences in people. Mother wanted us to understand, respect and value our neighbors. As children we experienced the broader world through these friendly, timeless encounters.

A neighborhood boy, Johnny, found a dead blue jay smack on the wooded path where we rode our bikes. What to do with it?

Mom told us kids, "Bring it to Brenda."

Being the youngest of the clan of kids who congregated on summer evenings to play games and cruise the neighborhood on our assorted wheels, I couldn't fathom what Brenda could do with a very dead bird. We delivered it to Brenda's doorstep.

A few weeks later, we returned and knocked on her cabin door. In her hands stood an upright, white skeletal bird form, securely fastened to a piece of wood. She presented it to us. I stood in awe. It even had a written inscription of the date, place, and who found it.

Pure magic to my eyes. Brenda certainly knew how to encourage our young inquisitive minds.

As I grew, I realized that Brenda Putnam was a most humble and gentle person who was a very talented and professional sculptress. Of course she knew how to assemble that bird's skeletal structure.

Years later I attended the NYC Metropolitan Museum of Art to enjoy the exhibits and enlighten my soul. As I exited an elevator, I gazed upon assorted bronze sculptures before me. My eyes glanced to read the artist's name: Brenda Putnam. Oh, my! Brenda, our very own dear neighbor.

IN HOPE

Karyl J. Leslie

I am now alone awhile.
Window's sunshine makes me smile.
Skies have shown a lot of gray,
but now the sunshine has its way.
I have work that I must do.
I pray that God will see me through
with guidance clear and help that's strong.
Then we can join to sing along
with affirmation from our souls,
which long always to be made whole.

As we seek to learn from God,
we find the Spirit helps to prod
our souls and beings, our minds, too,
our hearts, our bodies, toward a new
integration with the One
whose will we pray is always done
because that will is always best
and can withstand every test.

If we hang in long enough,
even when the way seems rough,
in the end we'll see anew
all the good that God can do.
When we offer God our lives,
we'll find we ultimately thrive.

A SKUNK AT THE COUNTY FAIR

Dennis F. King

Every year people gather to relax, be entertained and eat all types of exotic foods at Country Fairs across America. Where else can you find fried pickles, buffalo burgers, funnel cakes, deep-fried Oreos, as well as fresh, squeezed lemonade, hot apple cider, and Moxie flavored ice cream? The whole purpose of these local gatherings is to enjoy the warm weather, wearing shorts, rubbing elbows with neighbors and less frequently seen friends.

The names of the Fairs change if you travel around to enjoy the different themes like an Agricultural Fair, a County Fair, and the Country Fair. These events are held yearly, some for over a century. Judges taste home-baked goods; spectators watch sheep shearing, chuckle at the prettiest sow contests and some participate in the wife carrying races.

There is no limit to the excitement felt by young and old as the Fair day arrives. Families gather up the kids, Grandparents, and friends. They pull out that money tucked away for just this special occasion. The smells fill the air as dozens of food booths try to draw you in to taste their delights, but you are already eyeing the next snack on your list waiting to jump into your belly.

The word "diet" is rarely thought about or even mentioned. There's always room for more, and you get to walk it off. It's a place where adults of all ages can find something fun to look at, learn new things. This place is so important that even the little ones understand who is really in charge here and it is not them. Children may cry, make demands, stomp their feet, make faces but nothing works, Mumma and Daddy are too happy to notice their crocodile tears.

Fairs of the past often had an old, circular dirt racetrack for locals racing their horses or parading them around in beautiful dressage demonstrations; giant oxen pulls, pig scrambles and always the Saturday Night Demolition Derbies. Adventurous women, like my friend Kathleen the School bus driver by day, jump into her big, old pink "bomber" and competes in the "Powder Puff" Main Event.

They fire up their engines, sit on their horns, wave at the family one last time before the dainty hanky is dropped. The time for Ladies Tea with Crumpets suddenly ends and rear-enders, smashed fenders and blown engines are everywhere until one car is left moving. The crowds go crazy with hoots, howls, wolf whistles and plenty of laughs with a big ribbon pinned on the winner and a cash prize to boot. Some women are shocked, others shook up after losing but they walk tall, and the guys gain new respect for them, never to want her mad behind the wheel.

This all occurs almost overnight, we arrived on Tuesday morning to an empty, giant fairgrounds and started setting up our spot each year. It is quiet for the first couple of hours when suddenly, little convoys go rolling by us. All at once empty barns, wooden food booths and bare spots get brought to life with activity. The pace is fast, and like a yearly ritual, each person understands what must be finished by Thursday morning when the crowds start showing up.

We always set up next to The Flying Wallenda Family, the 6th, 7th and 8th generation of performers on the High-Wire, Trapeze, Jugglers and other feats of astonishment. The father Tino and his son Alex do most of the setting up of the rigging and a wire, over twenty-five feet above the ground. They never use a net below as they walk, bicycle, stand on chairs and do three-man pyramids to the roar of the crowds. They also stand on their heads and Tino, the Grandfather, has his five-year-old Grandson on his shoulders, stopping on the wire where the boy raises his arms, slowly.

I wandered over to talk to them during the day to say hello and pay my respects to this awe-inspiring family. Today Alex and his beautiful wife Claire are working together setting up the many cables and wires they need to perform. They have three Chihuahuas, one is older about 13 years old, and the other two are still pups and very active, I might say they are high strung. They seemed to bark at everything, but dogs do that when a stranger is nearby, or they smell something we do not.

Later that evening I settled down for the night on my Army fold up cot and had a quilt on me with a plastic tarp over that, we had to rough it until the trucks get emptied. Tonight it is outside in the fresh air as the whole camp settles in for some much-needed peace and quiet. Each of us has a little snack nearby to make for some sweet dreams and float away in dreamland, far from these woods but we are not alone. I turn on my cell phone and play the same Willy Nelson video. Ain't it funny how time just slips away, it is like a sleeping pill to me. I listen to each word and feel them; my eyes are glued to his fingers on the frets as a master performs. My coworker said, "Oh no, not more of that Hillbilly music?" He is Vietnamese, younger and more into Rap, crap. I was annoyed and told him to shut up, leave me alone.

Then all three Wallenda dogs started barking in unison. I imagined they were outside to do their business before their bedtime. I began to bark back at them in my best Pomeranian voice. It was funny and the more it broke the silence, the more I laughed. The dog owners certainly did not want their "babies" bothering the whole Fair Grounds, but sound does carry at night. My coworker Huong said, "You love to start trouble, Mr. King" I laughed and had to agree, but for the sake of everyone, I went back to Willy.

It was only ten minutes later when Huong is yelling at me "Mr. King, Mr. King, look, look, look!" I uncovered my head and looked towards him. He was about thirty feet away on his cot, but his eyes were wide open and looking at the ground in between us. There on the ground was the last of his Whoopie Pie being devoured by one of the original Fairgrounds' residents. When the dust of the day settled, this visitor came out of a borough, chased by Wallenda dogs and found a sweet snack.

I started to bang my cane against a tree while yelling, "HEE-YAH" and "Here Kitty Kitty, Kitty, HEE-YAH." Then it ran towards Huong's bed. He jumped up, grabbed a broom and started swinging it wildly, as the critter became trapped in a corner and put its tail up. We both froze for a long minute when our nocturnal visitor, a Skunk, turned to look at us. I played dead, and Huong calmly lit a cigarette. The beast took off into the dark, back towards the Wallendas. But I did not sleep well that night, would you?

In the morning, nary a scent of our nocturnal visitor. So I surmise that even the Fairgrounds nearby wildlife look forward to the annual attractions and tasteful distractions, not only the avid fairgoers.

MAGICAL CREATURES

Steven Michaels

They start out no bigger than a gnome.
The embrace of their leprechaun-like hand
is worth its weight in gold.
Their midnight shrieks can rival a banshee
while their coos can melt the hardest of hearts.

In learning to crawl, they stumble like a unicorn foal.
Upon walking, they start in on their impish ways—
veritable gremlins getting into everything.

Learning to babble in enchanted tongues is where
the real magic begins:
conjuring monsters from within the bed chamber,
hosting tea to a multitude of sprites,
slaying dragons unseen,
amidst a sea of giants.

Their power is boundless.
Their wisdom as matchless as the sage.
As untiring as a vampire,
Sucking the life force from you,
howling and making mischief
Both day and night,
And yet, in watching them grow
they place the stake upon your heart.

Then like fleeting pixie dust
they vanish in their way.
Morphing and changing
with bellow and rage,
developing a witch's skin
of pustules and pocks,
leaving their cherub faces far behind.

In old age, we see them from afar.
No longer resembling their fairy kind.
The once juvenile beast
having sojourned from out of its cave
blends into the rest of mankind,
never to be seen again.

A CAT BY ANY OTHER NAME

Sharon A Harmon

One of my friends told me that my neighbor who put food out for the wild turkeys that came into their yard, often saw a little black and white kitten that would follow them eating what the turkeys missed. That's crazy, I thought until a few weeks later as I talked on my phone in my kitchen gazing out the window into the woods. I saw a flock of turkeys trot down the mountain to my neighbor's house and just as my friend said there was a little black and white kitten following them. I couldn't believe my eyes.

A few weeks later he showed up on our front deck. He was getting bigger. My husband gave him a bowl of food, leery about how wild he might be. By his third trip to our deck, my husband was able to get him into the house. He was even bigger and he was solid as a block and his teeth looked incredibly sharp. We named him Bonehead. We put flea powder on him, combed him and fed him. He stayed a few weeks as a part of our family and was very friendly to us. One day he meowed to go out, we let him out and he disappeared.

We called neighbors to see if they saw him anywhere. The Edwards, our neighbors a mile away at the end of our dirt road, had seen him. "Oh you must mean Johnny Cat. That's our name for him, he comes to live with us for a few weeks too and then he disappears for a while before he comes back. We figured he liked it here because we own the farm and there's lots of mice in the horse's hay. He also goes a half a mile away to the Andersons and when they found him they took him to the vet and got him his shots and a checkup," she told us.

"We found out that they named him Hunter, now you two seem to be on his list."

A few months later Bonehead was back to us. We let him in. He was pretty beat up, with cuts, oozing wounds and a tiny piece of ear missing. He must have ran into some critter in the woods. It could have been a fox, raccoon, coyote or fisher cat, we'll never know.

My husband cleaned him up, put antibiotics on him and nursed him back to health. He gave him special treats and lots of love. Bonehead followed him from room to room like a puppy dog. He sat in his lap and purred. We tried to use cat toys, like strings and balls, but to no effect. He just sat there. When we thought about it we realized that being homeless and having to strive so hard to survive, he had probably never known the concept of someone playing with him like most other kittens. So we gave up on that and just loved him. Our daughter took a picture of Bonehead and framed it and gave it to my husband for Christmas, it brought tears to his eyes when he saw it. We considered him a part of our family.

Then Bonehead disappeared again for a long stretch of time. We drove around looking for him but to no avail. Weeks went by. One night we headed up to the town library five miles away. Heading up a big hill called Jacob's Ladder I saw a black and white cat sitting on a rock by the side of the road. "Wait, stop and back up!" I said. "I just saw Bonehead." And indeed it was. I got out of the car and called to him and he came running to me. I scooped him up in my arms. We were ecstatic and we brought him home again. We couldn't believe he had traveled that far. He stayed another day. Then he went out and we never saw him again.

We called the neighbors who were so fond of him, but no one had seen him. They were sad also. That cat was a true survivor he really seemed to have nine lives or at least three. Weather you called him Johnny Cat, Hunter or Bonehead he brought a lot of love into our lives and apparently into the lives of others who took him in. We hoped we had brought some love into his hard life. None of us would ever forget him, guess he moved on to cat heaven, where I imagine he has many, many friends.

A THREE-DOG LIFE

Diane Kane

I've lived a three-dog life. I know others who've had more, but three is enough for me. Growing up I never had a dog, but after I got married, I said to my husband, "I want a dog that looks like Ol' Yeller."

Bear was a yellow lab puppy with paws of great expectations. He was my constant companion through the unbearable heat of the summer of 1980 while I was pregnant with my first daughter. Bear and Shannon grew together, and he was the best big brother any little girl could have. Two years later, Danielle was born, and our family was complete.

Bear grew to be a giant of a dog, and like most big dogs, he didn't live long; ten years, not long enough. We buried him in our backyard with his toys and a piece of my heart.

Eventually, the girls wanted another yellow lab. Cody bounded into a house of active children and fit right in. He was nothing like Bear, but then no dog could be. I tried not to fall in love with him, but I failed. Cody was a social dog and an escape artist as well. We would come home from work to messages of Cody's escapades.

Cody died unexpectedly when he was nine years old. "Cancer," the vet said, although he'd never shown any symptoms. My husband dug the hole near Bear and gently placed Cody into it with his favorite blanket, all his toys, and another piece of my heart.

Several years passed, and we were dogless. I didn't think that I could love another. Then, our girls left for college, and the house took on a quiet that wouldn't go away.

"I need someone to greet me at the door with a wagging tail," I said to my husband.

Milo, half pug half beagle—Puggle—had a tail that won't stop; until one winter day when he was four years old. Milo jumped off our six-foot high deck and ruptured his back. We drove to the emergency vet through snowflakes and tears.

"You have two choices," the vet said. "We can perform a costly operation that might save him, or we can put him down."

The operation was long and complicated. Milo pulled through, followed by more than a year of successes and setbacks. My husband and I took turns with his daily physical therapy until he could finally walk on his own. Afterward, we agreed it was all worth it to see his little tail wag again.

Milo is twelve years old now. We reinforced the deck railings so he won't take that trip again. His legs still go out from under him when he gets too rambunctious, but it doesn't seem to bother him.

Sometimes I look at him and wonder, "how big will the hole in my heart be when he is gone?"

After all, it really doesn't matter. I'll always be thankful to have lived a three-dog life.

THE LURE

Michael Young

Starburst sun through
pine tree canopy,
slanted sideways beams
near dawn or dusk

illuminating leaf-green filigree
above
friendly waving ferns
below.

the soothing sound of
tea-dark water,
flowing through pools,
'round rocky rapids.

A heron poised stock-still
on a rock,
likes to fish alone.
A duck darts downriver,
not deigning to share the scene.

Visions of
leaping trout,
launching over my line
and the big one
I caught once

evaporate into
the foggy mist,
rising from the river.
It's time to go home.

I'll be back.

LADY, GO FIND THE GOATS!

Kay Deans

My heart stopped. There were no animals in the field—or in the barn—or for that matter, anywhere in sight when there definitely should have been five goats running toward me eager to be let out into the north field.

I walked around the barnyard and the adjacent Big Rock paddock looking for holes in the fence. But it wasn't a hole in the fence, it was an open gate. I had passed it twice before I saw it swing open on its hinge, the gateway to more than one hundred twenty acres of backwoods, of lush spring growth, filet mignon to the one-year-old goats who were AWOL.

I realized that trying to follow them would be a daunting task. Who knew what kind of lead time they had? And I would need help. So I trudged back through the barn and down the hill to the house to enlist the help of my husband Peter.

Alarmed, Peter said, "I definitely locked the gate last night. I remember doing it. I even double-checked it to make sure it was secure." We stared at each other, in suspension. Finally Peter finally broke the silence, "I'm going to find the goats. I'm taking Lady with me." Lady was our one-year-old German shepherd dog. German shepherds are good trackers and herders, but Lady had not been trained in either discipline. I was concerned that Peter was reacting to a horrible situation and not thinking clearly.

We had moved from the suburbs into the country one year prior, into an old farmhouse built in 1830 with ten acres of land, seven of which were woods. We wanted to clear some of the land and restore the fields, thus we enlisted the help of the five dairy goats. To protect them from predators and keep them in line, and because Peter grew up with German shepherds and loved them, we also got the dog. Lady was eight weeks old when she arrived on the farm. She spent her days side-by-side with the goats, keeping watch over them.

Peter leashed Lady and led her out. I followed. When we got to the field, I showed Peter how I had found the gate. Locking the gate is a two-step process that is supposed to prevent goats from opening the gate. First you slide a bar and then you flip a loop over a knob. We went through the gate and closed it behind us, but didn't flip the loop over the knob because we would be returning shortly.

Goats are browsers and they had left their browsing tracks all around us. Encouraged, we followed them for a short distance until the signs of their nibbling disappeared. That's when I turned around and stopped, my mouth agape. The gate was completely open. "Look Peter!" I said as I ran back to check it out.

Sure enough the gate had opened on its own. Mystery explained. When the loop wasn't fastened over the knob, the slide moved slowly downhill--nothing was level and the gate opened on its own. To fix it, the slide needed an uphill movement to open. We had built the gate backwards!

At least twice a day the goats watched us open and close the gates. They had mastered the first step in opening the gate as we thought they might, and gravity coupled with our inexperience as farm hands finished the job for them.

Even though we knew the solution to the problem, we might never have to use it because we didn't know how to find the goats. "These girls could be anywhere," I said. "They could run along the fences south or east and land in the road and get hit by a car or get someone killed. We have to notify the police and neighbors. I'm going back to call everyone."

Peter had explored this back end of our property and the neighbor's thirty-two adjoining acres and had described the layout of the land to me. "This way over to the west the land is a series of rocky ridges and pure woods, lots of underbrush, difficult to move around in," he said. "The land to the north is easier to traverse and there is a small apple orchard I know they'd love. They are probably there right now. I think I'll try that way."

I turned to leave and heard him say to the dog, "Lady, go find the goats."

My first phone call was to police dispatch who suggested I phone all the homes on both our road and the closest cross road a quarter of a mile away. I used the *Town Book of Residents* to identify names and the telephone directory to find their phone numbers. Everyone was concerned and willing to keep watch, but no one had spied any livestock. On learning I was new in town, several people tried to make me feel better by telling me about cows and horses that had gotten loose in the past (all had returned home safely).

I kept trying to convince myself that this was the best use of my time, that I truly was mobilizing people who could help in the rescue effort, that at some point the goats would have to emerge from the woods, and that one of these people would see them and rescue them before they got hit by a car.

Forty-five minutes later as my efforts were winding down Peter, his face white and drawn, returned home.

"The police are sending a cruiser to circle the area and keep an eye out for the goats," I said. "Everyone I reached by phone is watching for them."

"Well," Peter said, "I did a stupid thing. I unleashed Lady and told her to go find the goats. She trotted off due west into the brush and over the ridge. But the orchard is to the north and that's where I really thought the goats would go, so that's where I went. No sign of anyone at the orchard. I thought Lady would follow me, but she didn't. So now not only have we lost the goats, we've lost the dog."

I immediately called dispatch and told them about the dog.

"You know," Peter said, "I thought the goats would go to the clearing because I knew it was there—like they would know also. Stupid. How could they know? And I told Lady to go and find the goats because German shepherds are good trackers and I thought she would lead me to them. But I didn't follow her lead. Besides, like you said, she's not trained to track and find. Now she's lost too and it's my fault. I'm going back to find Lady. I'm going the way she went."

I tried to talk Peter into resting a bit first, but he was adamant. "Our only chance is now, not later."

"OK," I said. "But I'm going with you. We're taking the cell phones and a chain we can leave at the gate to secure it." We left the house.

From the gate we walked west but not in a straight line the way Lady went. We had to walk around several large rocks and fallen trees. We climbed the first ridge, looked around and called, "Lady! Laaaaady! Come!" Waited. No Lady. We were deep in the woods and could no longer see the road to get our bearings. In our haste, we had not thought to bring a compass. We could only hope we were still going in the right direction.

We trudged on, down the hill and up the second ridge calling, "Laaa dyyy! Come!" We stopped to catch our breath and called again. The forest floor was spongy with a deep layer of rotting vegetation that disguised treacherous rocks. I tripped and fell. I have advanced rheumatoid arthritis with several fragile joints and at that time had a newly replaced knee. We feared I would also end up needing to be rescued and debated turning back. While we waited to see if I was OK, we kept calling, "Laaa dyyy! Laaa dyyy! Come!" Still no Lady.

We decided to continue up and over the third ridge, walking a bit slower and more carefully. Anxiety began to show in our calls. When we reached the bottom before the fourth ridge, Peter said "I want to go back. I'm tired. We've come a long way and I'm worried about the effort it will take to get home. I hope I can make it."

Only one-year prior Peter had had his second heart attack and was still weak. The stress of the situation had started to show even before we began our 'Lady trek.' Now it had reached its peak. I hoped we hadn't waited too long to return home. "You rest a while. I can climb this ridge," I said. "If I don't see them, we'll go back together."

Peter found a rock and I found a fallen tree trunk to sit on. The woods were quiet. The breeze didn't reach this deep, and it was too early for black flies and mosquitoes. In a few more weeks the emerging leaves would completely hide the outline of the ridge. I got ready for the climb.

I had taken my first two steps up the ridge when we heard a rustling sound. I turned and we looked at each other both mouthing the same word, "Bears?" It was early spring, and these backwoods were bear territory. We were so focused on Lady and the goats. We had never given bears a thought. Now we did. We also realized that we hadn't told police dispatch about our plans, and even though we had our cell phones, we hadn't checked for reception. No one knew we were in these woods.

We stood, frozen in place. More rustling, sounding closer. We looked up and there was Sandy—one of the five goats! And Lady close behind her! Sandy ran downhill to where we stood. Lady circled us, returned to the top of the ridge, and disappeared.

Shortly, two more goats—Brownie and Whitey—appeared running downhill to us. Lady followed them, circled us, went back over the ridge. She came back with Blackie and Ollie, the final two goats. She circled Peter, me, and all five AWOL goats.

Peter and I laughed with relief. "Good girl, Lady. Good girl."

We began moving toward home, but it was slow going. Peter and I were tired. The goats took turns alternately walking so close to us that we were in danger of tripping over them and getting trampled and then roaming to taste the luscious vegetation. Lady all the while was circling us and returning the stray goats to the fold, making sure they did not escape again.

It seemed an age before we got back to the farm, but we didn't care. Our spirits were high, and we had gotten our second wind. We kept marveling about Lady's herding talents and praising her. She had done as Peter had asked and had found the goats, and she had kept them together for more than two hours before she found us. None of the goats were injured.

Finally, when everyone was in the field we closed and latched the gate AND securely locked it with the chain. But Lady wouldn't stop. With her herding on auto pilot, she was a perpetual motion machine. She had a job and she was doing it with full concentration. It took some effort, but finally we got her attention and made her understand that she could rest. Proudly, she pranced back to the house with us praising her all the way. She took a drink, went to her bed, lay down, and slept.

That night she got her usual kibble, but we topped it with a juicy sirloin steak we bought specially for her. She had earned it!

OUT IN THE WOODS

(This may be sung to the tune of "Long, Long Ago")

Karyl J. Leslie

Out in the woods beneath tall oak trees
I love to be, peaceful and free.
There I relax and sing with the breeze.
I am alone, quiet, at ease.

Deep in the woods, life is good, nothing's wrong.
There I can rest and feel my best.
I can be still or laugh loud and long.
Sounds of the woods sing my heart's song.

So now and then I retreat to the place
Where I can be alone with me.
Far from the rush of a city's wild pace,
I go to meet me face-to-face

To learn again what deep dreams I hold,
What things I feel, what is most real.
When I return, I feel calm and, all told,
Have in the woods reclaimed my soul.

This poem originally appeared in *Sparkling Light: Poems of Wonder and Grace*

NOW HEAR THIS

Kathy Chencharik

"Mountains of medications?" Eighty-year-old Alice Alden laughed so hard, tears rolled down her wrinkled cheeks. "Why Henry," she said when she regained control. "You know I don't take *that* many pills."

Henry shook his head. Dropping the newspaper onto the kitchen table, he pointed to his ear. "Turn up your hearing aid, dear," he yelled.

"Oh," Alice said as she turned up the volume. "What?"

"Mountains and meditations, that's what I said. It's the title of the next Quabbin Quills anthology. You wrote a story that was published in their first book called *Time's Reservoir*. Remember?"

"What time's the reservation?" Alice smiled. "Where are we going?"

"Probably to the nursing home if you don't get a new hearing aid," Henry shouted. "No reservation. Reservoir. *Time's Reservoir* the book!"

"Why didn't you say so? I really liked that one. What about it?"

Henry sighed. He got up out of his chair, walked around the table and sat beside his wife. Taking a deep breath he spoke loudly and directly into her ear. "I just read in the paper that the Quabbin Quills are going to put out a new book called *Mountains and Meditations*. I thought you might like to submit a story to that one too."

"Of course I would," Alice said. "But what should I write about?" She gazed into his deep brown eyes, peering out at her from behind a pair of thick glasses. Putting her hand on top of his head, she stroked the remaining tufts of white hair. "Henry, I do believe you are going bald."

Henry stood up. He brought his empty coffee cup over to the sink and stood with his back toward her. "No wonder I'm going bald," he whispered. "You're the reason I pull my hair out by the roots."

"Roots?" Alice asked. "You want me to write about our family roots?"

Henry turned to face her. Oh, great, he thought. She can't hear me when I look at her and yell, but with my back to her she can hear me whisper. "You heard that?" he asked.

"Heard what?"

"Never mind." Henry slowly shook his head. "Write whatever you want. But I'm going to call and make an appointment for you. It's time you got a new hearing aid."

BENEATH MY FEET

Liz Day

Beneath my feet is the gravel.
The sand.
The dirt between my toes.
The energy of mother nature flowing.
Flowing through my body
My legs
My heart
My lungs
My head.
It hums a song.
A song I am familiar with.
The song is mine though.
We each have our own.

It is a song of Love,
Dreams
Defeat
Triumph
Passion
Will.
The will to continue on this journey.

It flows through my veins thumping.
It calls to me.
It awakens me.
...It IS me.

It's time to put one foot in front of the other to continue this song

To move with the beat.

To Love.

To RUN

TOGETHER WE BUILD

Sonya Shaw Wirtanen

Jeff's long white hair is pulled back into a messy ponytail and covered by an oversized sun hat. His back hangs harshly forward, requiring his gaze to turn upward from under the comforting shade of his hat when he speaks. He is free on Saturdays and surprisingly prefers email instead of a phone call when his time is requested on the job. He is often the first one there and the last to leave. The dull black rain boots that he wears, have tread through the muddy dense soils of Pahoa. He knows that although the sun is out now, at any point the skies could open and unleash heavy rain onto us all. He wears his boots and his hat defining the difference between the locals and the expats. Jeff arrives happily with his toothless smile ready to work and ready to help. He is a retired carpenter and holds that title with pride, but not arrogance. The smooth curvature of his heavy wooden hammer holds the evidence of sweat and blood that has gone into building homes in the heat of the sun and wet of the rain for so many years. He joins us on Saturdays to quietly work and proudly serve the island which he calls home.

Beth arrives with her fiancé, Isaaic who, you can see immediately, is her best friend. They have the kind of relationship that holds the passion of their age, but the depth of their experiences. For many months, they came and went with small talk in between. Smiling for photos, completing any job that needed to be done without question or complaint.

After a while, we begin to get to know the regulars, but I don't think we are ever prepared to know their stories. I knew Beth was young, but I never thought I had nearly ten years on her. She and Issaic have seven children. Seven children whom they have raised, and now unconditionally love. Some from birth, others from childhood, but each and everyone calls them Mom and Dad. Their minivan holds their pride and their story with every cheerio on the floor, each car seat safely buckled in the back, and the thin white stick figures joyfully placed on the back window. 1,2,3,4,5,6,7... seven children who they never know when they will lose, when they will be taken back to the dark life they were saved from. Between the bed time stories, the doctor's appointments, the visits from the state and the biological mom, between the laundry and grocery shopping, the kisses and the tears, they come out to the job site to volunteer their time, to serve even more people. After working on the build site, I watch Beth and Issaic venture off together to the shelter where they sort food and clothes for the volcano evacuees. They know in their hearts they still have more to give and that many are still suffering. It's no wonder, so many keys hang from the loop of Beth's belt buckle; each one connected to another heart and another life entrusted in her care.

As for Kent, they told me it had been ten years since he walked onto the job site to lend a hand. They informed me that he would be there three days a week, refusing to take a thing in return. Kent is not the tallest man you will meet. His Japanese heritage shows through in his stature and his accent. He often leaves out the ending of words and talks in quick short sentences, leaving me unsure but confident that what he said was wise and true. He laughs often, usually from his own jokes. For ten years he insists the women take their plates before him and he refuses to sit while he eats. Referring to younger members as Sir, he listens attentively to the next direction and next assignment. No wife, no children, just a man who so humbly comes and goes, day after day, to do his part to leave this world better than it was when he arrived into it. Kent is why the word Ohana is so often used around here.

Adam works hard swinging his hammer but is easily distracted by the broken glass next to this tiny respite that he helped to build. He sits cross-legged on the ground, in his shorts and boots, and begins to pick up the glass piece by piece. Evelyn joins him, then James and lastly me. We talk about kava and taro, the difference between a WOOFER and somebody who lives in *community*. Eventually we talk about his van that he now calls home since he lost his cottage, his farm, and his life in the wrath of Pele, the Goddess of Fire, who took back her land in the eruption of Kilauea.

We work together for weeks, building tiny houses on land donated by the church. From foundation to framing, to roof and to railings, we build these homes to get families out of tents and off of wet pallets.

One day, I sneak off the job site to surprise the volunteers with some coffee. I don't have to go far, just around the corner to a place called The Tin Shack, which looks exactly the way it sounds. The rusted tin of the roof and walls unevenly falling purposely into one another. Outside the coffee shack, the smell of marijuana lingers undisguised by the women in tie dye skirts who are talking to the shirtless men hula-hooping outside the door. I proudly wear my own tie-dye shirt with Habitat for Humanity printed on the front. They give me a "shaka" and a nod thanking me for what we do. I return to the strangers who sweat the same as me and give them their coffees.

Kai likes to talk and takes this opportunity to express his gratitude for what we do. He is from Malachi but moved here eight years ago with his wife, so his daughter could go to college. He is now a mac nut farmer on the Big Island, but he is looking for work in carpentry because it pays a lot better than farming these days. Kai talks about Aina, the land in which we live. It is the land that is sacred and deserves our respect. He explains what peace means to him and the impact that kindness has on others. He is confident in the words he says, but he does not preach when he speaks about God.

People share their stories of why they are here and why they serve every day. Whether it is the teenager from Minnesota who excitedly explained on the flight here that this is his third mission trip to serve with YWAM, or the couple who travel on volunteer trips to give back even though the devastation that the opioid epidemic has had on their life back in New England would be enough to make them bitter and only think of themselves and their own suffering. Everyone has a story. I listened to a man who saved his money for the last ten years to build his dream home and retire in Hawaii so his wife who suffers from Parkinson's will have less stress and less flare ups from the debilitating disease...only to have his dream destroyed and burned to the ground eight months later by the eruption.

People from around the world and across the island come together, join hands in prayer, swing their hammers and share their stories with me. I think about what the Dalai Lama says, "joy is the reward, really, of seeking to give joy to others. When you show compassion, when you show caring, when you show love to others, in a wonderful way you have a deep joy you can get in no other way. You can't buy it with money. You can be the richest person on Earth, but if you care only about yourself, I can bet my bottom dollar you will not be joyful. But when you are caring, compassionate, more concerned about the welfare of others than about your own, wonderfully, wonderfully, you suddenly feel a warm glow in your heart, because you have in fact wiped the tears from the eyes of another."

While shingling a roof I met a girl from Romania who taught me about her culture and the proper use of the word, *Gypsy*. As I stood on a ladder brushing blue paint onto a house in the forest, I learned the struggles of a single dad who cares for his physically handicapped son, while he works harder than all of us to help himself into a new home that would have taken many more years to finish on his own. I have eaten lunch with a man from Afghanistan who was expecting his second child. He told me how he worries about his wife in all this heat and he hopes he can finish the addition on his house before the baby comes. Nearly every day we worked, we also listened. We heard the stories of joy, heart ache, courage and culture. These stories and these inspirational people that I met through this journey have discovered the meaning of life, and I am eternally grateful to have been given this gift of realization by them.

Selections from
CUTTING A BOND WITH THE LONG TRAIL
Entries & Poems by Ned Green compiled by his "ole ma" Clare Green

Day 15, October 8, 1997

Mountains rise out of primordial soup
in the fading yellow daylight
I see through windows without pane
Breezes lazily drift
no sounds except flatulence and far off cities
Suddenly, the A.T. exposes the world
outside the L.T. microcosm
we are dipping our selves into nothing
and realizing the magnitude of everything.

May all hikers (souls, soles) find peace on their TREK.

October 16, 1997

The smoke curls
Off hand rolled death
I write on the funk
live emanations of jive
the rain outside
cool and raw
an average fall
the pen escapes my hand
I am unknowing in pajamas
still not quite able
to wake up
jump out of the unconsciousness
into the future
Catalysts?
Drag your soul up above
the chainsaws and cars
to a realization
that we'll all be dead soon enough

FOR THE GREATER GOOD

Nancy Tatro

Take warning when those in powerful positions begin to spout rhetoric that sounds sensible in theory, especially when it alludes to the sacrifices of the few for the good of the many. It almost always means that those few will be getting the proverbial short end of the stick. Take, for instance, the creation of that beautiful body of water we call the Quabbin Reservoir.

I always considered myself to be well-read and moderately well-educated, so imagine my surprise upon learning that the phrase, "the needs of the many outweigh the needs of the few," wasn't penned by some philosopher, but by Harve Bennett for the 1982 *Star Trek* film titled, *The Wrath of Khan*. It was delivered by Leonard Nimoy as Spock. I pondered the phrase while thinking about how the Quabbin Reservoir was created. I was vaguely aware of the flooding produced to satisfy Boston's need for drinking water, but it wasn't until recently that I began to realize the sacrifices made and the injustices perpetrated to form the Quabbin.

Imagine being a resident of one of those towns destroyed to benefit residents of a city eighty-eight miles away. Residents of Dana, Endicott, Prescott and Greenwich lived in a seemingly idyllic valley. They were proprietors and workers that supported industry, farms, theaters, hotels, stores, cemeteries. In short, their days had all the trappings of a good, peaceful life...until the area was discovered by wealthy city folk. But even then, in the beginning at least, the attention was a boon to the economy of the area. To escape the heat and noise of summer, many city dwellers vacationed in Western Massachusetts.

But the tables turned.

The trouble began when Boston could no longer supply sufficient potable water for its approximately 800,000 residents.

Created in 1919, the Metropolitan District Water Supply Commission met to decide how the water shortage could best be addressed. These hearings, primarily held in Boston many miles from the Quabbin area, would forever change the lives of those in the four towns. Poor infrastructure and lack of motor vehicles made it difficult if not virtually impossible for most of the soon-to-be displaced people of central Massachusetts to attend and make their voices heard. It was probably not the first time and certainly not the last time that politicians and powerful wealthy people from Boston and its environs made decisions affecting the lives of those members of the commonwealth not fortunate enough to live close to the seat of government.

Perhaps the folks in the four lost towns heard sentiments similar to Spock's pronouncement. Or maybe politicians quoted Jeremy Bentham who posited that "it is the greatest happiness of the greatest number that is the measure of right and wrong." Did either of those statements justify taking the land, homes, and businesses of over two thousand people for pennies on the dollar? Could this statement truly legitimize not only depriving the living residents of their homes, but also exhuming some seventy-six hundred bodies and relocating them to a cemetery miles away?

Hard as it may be to believe, that is, in a nutshell, exactly what happened. The decision was made official in 1927 by the Metropolitan District Water Supply Commission. Just after midnight on April 28, 1938, the Winsor Dam stopped the Swift River's flow, flooding and destroying Enfield, Dana, Prescott and Greenwich to satisfy the needs of the many at the sacrifice of the mostly powerless and voiceless few.

I would like to think that such an event - dare I say travesty - couldn't happen again in Western Massachusetts to those who are far from the seat of power. It could happen anywhere in this country. I repeat my initial warning: be on your guard when you are among the few who will be sacrificing for the good of the many.

THE LOST TOWNS OF QUABBIN

Nancy Damon Burke

We were towns with homes,
churches, stores and schools.
Built by craftsmen and women
with bare hands and tools.

The seventeen hundreds
were wild and tough.
Small towns worked hard to
have simply enough.

"The British are coming"
was Paul Revere's cry,
We sent our militiamen,
many would die.

There were wars and rebellions.
Independence was new.
Villages became towns as
Massachusetts grew.

It was often a struggle
to live cradle to grave
in this land of the free
and the home of the brave.

There were whispers that Boston
needed water to drink.
That's not our problem

was all we could think.

They didn't know us,
the folks from the city.
They came out in the summer,
It was cooler and pretty.

We were glad when they came,
And when they were leaving
Their presence seemed gracious
But somehow deceiving.

Sure enough they decided
these towns were the place.
They would cover with water
And leave barely a trace.

In a matter of years,
we were told we must go.
A hundred and eight an acre
seemed surprisingly low.

For all they were taking
from us way out here,
To give to strangers
not neighbors, nor even near.

When the clock struck midnight
on that sad April day.
Enfield, Dana, Greenwich and Prescott,
just went away.

The roads, fields and pastures
to left and to right,
were covered with water
and soon out of sight.

High points and steeples
are lone islands now.

In the vast miles of water
you might wonder how.

If there wasn't a story
of how this came to be,
you'd guess only Nature
could create what you see.

But no, this was man
who took four towns away
and we're left to wonder;
could it happen today?

MARIGOLD VERONA MEETS MADAME PELE

Linda J. Donaldson

Marigold Verona lay in Brett's arms on the sunny beach in Hawaii. It had been an idyllic honeymoon, and she was so happy to be alive. They had arisen late, brunched at the resort, and taken their cuddly blanket out to the sand. She could hear the steady heartbeat of her beloved Brett as she rested her head on his chest—feeling the slippery suntan lotion between her cheek and his skin. Ah, *life is good*, she thought. *Dreams come true and life is good.*

"I can hardly wait to move into our new home in Warwick when we get back," murmured Brett. "I have plans to fix up that back porch for you."

"We are going to enjoy the woods and that big field in our side yard," she replied. "I have plans for bird feeders and a garden."

"Right now," Brett sighed. "I sure am enjoying this sunshine and the sound of the waves."

"Me, too." Marigold's voice was soft and she felt awash in contentment.

That same afternoon, they decided to take a drive along the Hamakua Coast. After stopping at Akaka waterfalls, enjoying a lush hike through the Hawaii Tropic Botanic Garden, they arrived at the Jaggar Museum.

They learned about the Kilauea Volcano and about Pele, the goddess of fire, who is known in the Hawaiian religion as the Creator of the Hawaiian Islands. Walking out of the Visitors Center onto the Overlook, they could clearly see the Halema'um'u crater in the center of the Kilauea Caldera.

By this time, the sun was setting and the glow from the crater was getting brighter. There were a few tourists still lingering to enjoy the sight when suddenly the earth began to rumble. A huge plume of flame and ash arose from the crater.

Brett and Marigold looked at each other as they gasped in amazement. When their gazes returned to the volcanic plume, they clearly saw a vision of long wavy hair topped by a tiara of tropical flowers. Her glowing eyes burned brightly as her gown of lava extended into the caldera.

"People of earth, hear me." She said. "I am Tutu Pele, Pele-honua-mea of the sacred land. I am Ka wahine 'ai honua, the earth eating woman."

Marigold was mesmerized—not sure if she were imagining this or experiencing it. She looked around and saw that Brett and the other tourists were equally enthralled by the sight of the shimmering lava plume.

"I am the daughter of Haumea, and I have a message for you." Her voice rumbled over the flat land between the overlook and the crater. "You have known me as She Who Shapes the Sacred Land, and I am your conscience."

Marigold reached for Brett's hand and they held on tightly. They listened, mouths agape.

"Know that earth has one crust," the voice announced. "Know that what you do under the water or atop the mountains affects every nook and crevasse of our planet. Know that the oil that flows beneath the crust is our blood and our life. If you drain the blood, the body cannot sustain itself. You know this and yet you allow the plunder to continue."

A loud rumble travelled up Marigold's legs and she could feel the earth's tremors in her heart. As the figure extended her arms, birds appeared to fly from her fingertips. Glorious plumage in yellows, oranges and reds fluttered into the sky and faded away.

"Although I devour the Island with molten lava, I also continuously create new land." The face of the volcano goddess wavered and flickered but the eyes were vivid and burned with passion. "You must care for the creatures of the sea and of the sky and of the sacred land, you must treasure each plant and each tree. Each leaf, each heart, each wingspan is dependent upon the continuation of the whole. Cherish your planet and act accordingly. Stop the plunder. Stop the degradation. You will not like the result if you do not heed my warning."

She moved her skirts and sea creatures rose and writhed at her feet, reflecting the sparkling sunset in the drops of water that splashed around them. The other tourists gasped as the dazzling sight dissolved.

As the plume of ash wafted away on the wind and the pillar of flames subsided, the vision within the fire lingered in the eyes of those who had beheld this mystic moment. Darkness had fallen on the overlook and the stars appeared as a tapestry above the expanse of desolation. All looked up and contemplated the message they had received. Each person had been touched by this encounter. Some were moved profoundly and were forever changed. Others shook it off and, not trusting their own perceptions, dismissed it as a moment of imagination.

Brett and Marigold discussed the vision on their ride back to the resort, over dinner and on the beach during the following days. This same discussion continued as they jetted homeward to begin their lives as a married couple.

"Did you see what I saw?" Brett asked for the tenth time, still flabbergasted.

"I saw a beautiful woman defending her planet," Marigold reiterated. "I saw Pele and her creatures of sky and sea. I stood beside you while we witnessed a proclamation of mythic proportion."

Brett was still assuring himself that he hadn't had a solitary hallucination.

"Whew!" he told her, "I'm glad we both saw it or neither of us would have believed it!"

One Saturday morning a few months later, Brett and Marigold were in their sunny breakfast nook going over the mail.

"Here's my new membership card for the Environmental Defense Fund," Brett said as he opened an envelope. "I forgot to mention that I'd joined."

Marigold laughed. "I'm expecting my card from The Nature Conservancy any day now!" They grinned at each other remembering the beautiful face of Madame Pele and the wise words that flowed from her lips of lava that magical evening during their honeymoon.

"Let's go to Mount Grace today!" They said simultaneously.

SPIRITUS MUNDI

Steven Michaels

Last night I dreamt
of spring
but not in opposition
to the cold.

A figure came
slouching toward me.
He appeared broken
bleeding from the side
carrying a platter,
serving up a hog's head.
Its mouth swollen with an apple.

The figure wept until
the apple fell away
And I was set free--

I awake to
seasons upended
and the realization
our brethren are dead inside
and bleeding.
Our dignity is served up by the head
through internal affairs and human vice.
Therefore, we must upturn the tables.
Stop the hate crimes in the temple.
Stop the hate before the crime.

Let he who is without
build a wall
then call up Jericho--
its people will know
what to do
and I'll go
back to sleep
to dream
to bide my time
just as Jesus would do
before a second coming.

HUBRIS

James Thibeault

As he tried to ignore the endless howls and hollers of high school sophomores entering his classroom, Terrance Spencer—the long-time English teacher—asked himself why this class felt so tragically Greek. Of course, teaching Greek mythology this semester was the obvious explanation, but his personal experience with these students felt something out of the mythos.

Spencer took a deep breath to try and calm his nerves. Instead, he breathed in the sweaty, adolescent stench of defiance. Dozens of students clowned around as though they were on the playground—their laughter bitter and caustic. A kid in the back made bird noises.

Why is he even … it doesn't matter.

A paper suddenly flew in the air. With all the commotion, it was difficult to find the point of origin. Spencer didn't feel like playing the "who threw that?" game.

Just start class, he thought, *and end this pandemonium.* He ran a hand through his hair. Spencer felt like he was a joke of a teacher. Other teachers had complete control over their students. Or, was that a myth too? Was the perfect class just as plausible as the Golden Fleece? Dionysus had seemed to possess the students' spirits—they were drunk with foolishness.

"Alright, settle down please." Spencer tried to sound authoritative. Some sat down in their seats, while many continued talking. He cleared his throat and tried again, his voice slightly sterner. No response—the others continued talking with no regard to him.

Spencer's attention focused on Susan—one of the few students who didn't seem crazy. She sat down and looked over her notes.

Why did she have to be so abnormal?

Out of a whole class, only a few seemed to understand what you actually did at school. Spencer thought that all he had to do was to teach something memorable. He thought that if he could be respectful and make them laugh, they would grow to enjoy his company. That was him being arrogant—believing that he once had the incredible talent to teach. Alas, it was *hubris*: confidence that horribly backfires.

Teaching required grit, like Odysseus and his grueling quest to get home. He wasn't Odysseus, that man literally went through hell and back to get what he wanted. At this point, Spencer wanted to stay on Calypso's island and give up. The kids relentlessly wore him down. He constantly felt challenged to fight, like Achilles against Hector in front of the walls of Troy. When he first began teaching, Spencer pictured himself to be Achilles—an unstoppable force with the marker as his sword. After years of bearing the strain of education, Spencer was more of a Hector—one who knew his own downfall before the combat began, yet bravely tried his best to win.

It seemed that Spencer accepted the Fates' dooming decree yet endured another pathetic teaching day. However, Hector's plight was noble and poetic, while Mr. Spencer's attempt to teach his students Greek Literature felt pathetic.

He watched one girl tag Susan's neck with a marker, a boy scrawling the word "dumb" all over his textbook, and Harriet screaming because José kept kicking the back of her legs.

"José, stop! I mean it. Seriously," shrieked Harriet. The rest of the class looked over in interest.

José smirked and kicked her again.

"What?"

"Oh my God. Just stop!"

"Make me."

Harriet looked over at Spencer with pleading eyes—this same girl had yelled at him last week because she didn't think she deserved a

34 on her Iliad exam. Spencer asked her if she studied. She said the notes were too boring. Now, he was suddenly useful to her.

"Mr. Spencer, he's kicking me. Make him stop."

Spencer let out a sigh. "José, can't you stop kicking her please?"

"But I wasn't doing anything."

"You did it right in front of me. I would like you to stop." Spencer said it as calmly and respectfully as he could. It didn't matter.

"I don't know what you are talking about," José said, puzzled. Perhaps he actually forgot what he just did—drinking from the river Lethe.

Spencer's fist clenched as he held in a scream. He had to keep his cool. If he yelled, the kids would win. It was a constant struggle to remain in control whilst enduring the barrage of disrespect. Class hadn't even started yet, and he was already longing for the bell.

"José, would you mind moving to that seat over there?"

"But why?"

"Please, just do——"

"This is so unfair!"

"Now!" Spencer raised his voice, and the class fell silent. Unexpected peace reigned for a second. Peace, from aggression.

Why was this the only way to get to some of the children?

Perhaps they longed for glory in battle and here, in this student stadium, was the place to hone their skills. This reminded him of Achilles, who had a chance to live a safe and comforting life but declined it—choosing the lust for battle instead.

"Whatever," José mumbled. He grabbed his books with nostrils flaring and walked across to the other side of the room. Slamming the books on the ground. Spencer couldn't bear it but sadly let it go. Already, too much time had been wasted. He would be lucky if he even finished his lesson today.

"You know," Harriet said, raising her hand—completely missing the point of hand-raising. "You didn't have to yell at José —we were just joking around."

"Exactly," mumbled José.

"It doesn't matter. You just don't do that in a classroom. Anyway, let's *finally* start class."

Spencer turned around to write on the board and immediately the students started talking. It began as a whisper, but soon the students grew confident and roared into conversation. Barely finishing a sentence, Spencer turned around and released a *shhh* from his lips. It didn't work.

"Okay, okay." Spencer weakly ordered, "Back to me."

Most of the students settled, but there were a few scattering blasts of giggles. Spencer stared at the girls in the back until they stopped. The technique worked, but it just wasted even more time. For a moment, he completely forgot what he was going to say. He finally had the class' attention and drew a blank.

Focus, he said to himself. He remembered. "We talked yesterday about Odysseus visiting the Land of the Dead, and Homer mentions a man named Sisyphus."

A hand raised in the back. It was Bobby, the one who was chirping bird noises before.

"Yes?"

"Who's Homer, I thought this was about the Odyssey guy."

"Homer is the author," Spencer said with frustration.

"Oh," said Bobby. Susan smirked, and Bobby shot her a look. "What's so funny?"

"Nothing, we've only been reading this for a few weeks now."

"So?"

"Continuing," Spencer tried to refocus before the tension grew. "Sisyphus, by far, is my favorite Greek character because of the insane torture Zeus gives him."

"You like when people get tortured, that's really messed up." Interjected Harriet. Others murmured in agreement.

"Well, I'm not for torture per se, but more so the creativity behind Zeus. He punished Sisyphus for escaping the Underworld—in fact, it was wild what Sisyphus did. He somehow managed to shackle Hades—and then no one could die."

"That's impossible." Bobby squawked. "People have to die." He gave a smug look to Susan—proud that he said something intelligent.

"It's a myth. It's not supposed to be real," Spencer responded.

"So, if this is all fake, then why are we learning it?" asked Bobby.

The class roared in agreement.

"Because it's important to understand different stories outside of your own. It helps you better appreciate the world."

"Mr. Spencer," continued Bobby, "Yesterday, you talked about a cyclops named Polyurethane."

"Polyphemus."

"Whatever, the point is—before I was rudely interrupted—that no one believes in these stories. Cyclopes don't exist, so this is dumb."

"How is that an argument?"

"Are you serious? Zeus, Hades, Aphrodisiac, Zeus—they're all fake, and you're making up some non-real stories. There is only one God, and that God is Jesus." Bobby blew a kiss to the sky. Everyone clapped.

Why were they clapping?

"Oh, my bad. After all …" said Spencer with sarcasm. He felt himself slipping. *Keep in your anger, they feed off your frustration. Don't crack.* Spencer didn't finish his thoughts. Harriet's hand shot up.

"Mr. Spencer, why didn't you finish your sentence?"

"What are you talking about?"

"The way you said 'Oh, my bad.' What were you going to say back to Bobby?"

"It doesn't matter."

"We're listening," said José in the back. "What were you going to say to Bobby?"

Spencer took a deep breath, recollected his thoughts. He might as well be honest with the students. Wasn't that what they wanted?

"All I was going to say is that myths appear in all religions. If you critique ancient Greek religion, then you need to do the same for Christianity as well."

Bobby's eyes widened. "Wait, are you saying that God isn't real?"

"What? No, I'm just—"

"So you don't believe in God? Is that what you're saying?" José cocked his head to the side. Achilles had rallied his troops, and they were ready for war.

"He's teaching us this Greek stuff to convert us!" yelled Bobby.

The class collectively gasped. *Were they serious?* It was hard to tell.

"Really?" said Susan. Her palms raised in exasperation. "Will you cut-out all of this shit? Just let him teach!"

"Mr. Spencer, Susan just said 'shit'!" Bobby pointed an accusatory finger.

"Don't say that word," said Spencer.

"What word?"

"You know."

"But she said 'shit'!"

"Stop saying 'shit'!" Spencer snapped. The class giggled. He had lost again. Administration would hear how he swore in class. It would be an awkward conversation, and there was no point in explaining it. Every response from administration was the same: "All of this could have been avoided if you were more reasonable with the students."

Instead of yelling at Bobby, he conceded. Breathing in what seemed like the entire room, Spencer collected himself once again. *Don't lose your cool*, Spencer thought. *Get back to the lesson.*

"Moving on," Spencer suddenly said with fake cheer, "Since no one could die, Ares was furious—what's the fun of war if no one dies? Ares releases Hades and Sisyphus is sent back to the Underworld. There, Sisyphus awaits his punishment, which was maliciously designed by Zeus." Spencer paused for a moment—expecting a barrage of noise from students. They were silent—all eyes were on him. Spencer felt a sudden wave of excitement. This feeling, complete engagement with his students, was intoxicating. He had felt as though he just consumed ambrosia—feeling the strength of the Gods. Everything before did not matter; it was this moment that he cherished. Real learning was being transmitted into their skulls; he could feel it. He was teaching, helping these students enrich their lives. Spencer spoke with more confidence—swaying to his own rhythm—speaking with conviction. "Prometheus had his liver devoured by birds. Ixion was bound to a burning wheel. And what was Sisyphus' evil punishment?" Spencer baited the eager students for a moment. "He had to push a boulder up a mountain."

"That's all?" said Susan.

"Sounds easy, right?"

"Was it like a flaming boulder or something?" questioned Bobby.

"Nope."

"So, there has to be a catch, right?" added Harriet.

Mr. Spencer smiled.

"Great job, Harriet. That's exactly it." Spencer suddenly smirked, unable to contain his excitement. "See, he would have to push this boulder up a mountain, but just as he reaches the top—ever so close to victory—the boulder would then fall backwards. It would roll all the way back down, and he would have to start all over again. Forever."

"So, he can never reach the top?" said Bobby.

"He'll try, for eternity, but he never will make it."

The class took a pregnant pause—ruminating the moment. *Please, let this last, just for a few moments longer.* Tragically, it didn't.

José broke the silence. "How can he push a boulder up a mountain if he's in the Underworld?"

"Well, that's a great question. The Underworld has a lot of fantastical elements, like rivers that make Achilles immortal, giant three-headed dogs, and—"

"How about you just answer my question. There's no way you can have a mountain in an underground cavern."

"I was getting to that, and I would appreciate it if you stop the attitude."

"Now you're just dodging the question."

"Fine, I think it was more of a hill."

"So, you were just lying to us?"

"It was a mistake, I apologize."

"Aren't you supposed to know all of this stuff? You can't even tell the difference between a hill and a mountain?"

Spencer took a deep breath, "I would appreciate if—"

"I feel bad for you, you know?"

"José, please—"

"I mean, this is it for you: this job."

"I'm giving you a warning, please don't get me—"

"And the worse thing is," José grinned, "You can't even do it right. You're just a bad teacher."

The class stared at Spencer, awaiting a counter. Spencer's eyes narrowed. If José wanted a war, he would give him a war.

Spencer ran up to him and screamed, "You listen here you little jerk." He pointed a finger in front of José's face. Nostrils flaring, face red—*aristeia,* the warrior rage of Mr. Spencer, had begun.

"You think I give a damn about you? You contribute nothing to this class and society. You are a problem, and do you know what people do with problems: they forget them. You will eventually fail out of this school and end up flipping burgers at two in the morning, and you won't even be able to do that right."

José was silent, then ever-so-slightly he leaned into Spencer. It was a whisper, but everyone heard it—it was that quiet. "Perhaps, but you'll still be here. So, who will have it better?" Spencer pulled back his fist. Achilles slaughtered a slew of Trojans, Odysseus massacred a hundred suitors—why couldn't he do the same? Spencer's fist shook, the veins in his forearm apparent. He wanted to pound José's face until it crumbled like Troy. Jose didn't move. "Do it, come on. Administration would love to hear this."

Spencer lowered his arm and let it fall dumbly to his side. He was no mythological figure, Spencer was real—and felt that was worse. The bell rang. Quietly, everyone stood up and walked out of the room.

José was the last to leave—staring Spencer down the whole time. When alone, Spencer kicked a chair with the strength of Sisyphus. Like a boulder, it fell to the ground. Mr. Terrance Spencer knew he would need to lift it back up before the next class arrived.

NIGHT

Jon Bishop

Dark now.
Only a whoosh of a car
outside my window,
or the distant screech
of an owl—or is it a bat?

No streetlights and no lights
in my room, and so the night
is like a womb, a cocoon,
enveloping my thoughts and me
totally in dark
and in silence,

like some antique contemplative,
one who rises before the sun,
sits in the black quiet
and stares straight ahead,
his eyes looking beyond his cell,
beyond his window and beyond
the night, the sky,
the trees, the birds,
the world.

INVISIBLE HITCHHIKER

Clare Green

A whirring sound came from behind me on Route 91 North as dusk approached. I neared Longmeadow, Massachusetts. The summer's day had filled me with the luxury of having visited dear friends in Greenwich, Connecticut. Two motorcycles sped by me in the passing lane. An uneasy feeling washed through me, so I sent a simple prayer from my heart after they had passed. My spiritual sensitivity and common sense acted like radar. It was too dangerous to have a high-speed game of chase on the interstate! In the moment, a subtle thought like a flash of sunlight in the dark forest, seemed to indicate that someone was about to die.

No more than five minutes down the highway, traffic slowed down. I knew what I might see. A moment later, chills coursed through my body, as I drove past the intense accident. Two motorcyclists had crashed, and one body was thrown onto the road. I sent love and light to them both and to the scene as I passed by.

I knew immediately that I had picked up the spirit form of the motorcyclist, like an "invisible hitchhiker." He was there sitting in my passenger seat, in his spirit form. In my thoughts I welcomed him. I told him what I had seen and what had happened to him. I told him to attend to the light and let his guardians in spirit help him. The tingling vibrations subsided from me and I knew that the silent hitchhiker had moved on. I wished him well. I wondered. I didn't know if he was killed instantly or just disoriented from his accident, but I tried to clarify to him what had occurred. The rest of my journey home was easy and uneventful.

Three days later, I was sitting comfortably at my kitchen table enjoying lunch when I felt ocean waves of energy run through my body and an accompanying silent presence. Inwardly, I asked who was near. I was amazed at the response. It was the invisible hitchhiker to whom I had offered help and conversed with in my thoughts a few days earlier. His presence was a surprise gift. His spirit came by simply to thank me and, in a whisper of a moment, the presence dissolved. My heart was smiling, and I was nourished well beyond the physical body that lunchtime. I thought, *be well, my hitchhiker friend and thank you for finding me.*

I reflected that it's never too late to say thank you, no matter the distance. Also that one must trust that thoughts are as deeds done. Once again, I was reminded how mysteriously infinite are the ways of energy. I appreciated that the hitchhiker found me to extend his appreciation. It helps fuel the cycle of life and affirm our interconnectedness. I respect the delicate gifts of clairvoyance bestowed and try to serve, attune and be mindful of what life bestows upon me.

It was as if a postcard from heaven had arrived that day to my table:

"Yo, Mamma Highway Driver! Made it to my next destination, thanks to your help! Super surprised where I landed 'cause thought I was headed elsewhere. Thanks again for directions and info. Your Invisible Hitchhiker Friend."

Upon reflection from this experience, I offer the following sensitivity exercise tip: Especially while traveling you may imagine a ribbon of golden light from you to your destination. That light will embrace you and everything within your journey. You will feel protected and become aware of happenstances along the way. Remain calm and serenely alert within the light of love as you travel. Breathe. Ready, set, go, on your trip!

STAN LEE, SOUTHWEST, AND SHAKESPEARE

Steven Michaels

Approaching 14,000 feet
her nervousness comes and goes
and I start thinking about Stan Lee.

Moments pass
my wife's head droops upon my shoulder
as our hands become more fastened
than our seatbelts
and I realize life's too short
to go it alone.

Suddenly
her head slides down a bit more
the air increasingly trembles.
If catastrophe should strike
we'd go out like Romeo and Juliet.
Or perhaps like Sue and Reed Richards
whose tragedy ended with superpowers.
I chuckle to myself
thinking how much Stan Lee
has become the new Shakespeare--
that *Two Gentlemen from Verona*
have been replaced by Thor and Captain America:
the singularity having something to do with capes.

At this altitude
It occurs to me how much the pen is my Mjolnir,
which, accompanied by her gentle breathing,
keeps me strong.

A sea of clouds bares us.
The seatbelt sign remains engaged.
Life no longer worries me:
here's to having lived it like
Stan, the Man, Lee.

PRIESTLY FRIENDS

Mary Louise Owen

Marrying Peter Clark, an Army officer, changed Katie Beth Wilson's life beyond imagination. Katie Beth Wilson had been raised in a sheltered religious environment in Washington State's emerald city, Seattle. However, Peter and Katie Beth's first assignment at an Army base in Central Massachusetts opened a world of new possibilities.

Over the years an unlikely relationship developed between Katie Beth and several different Army chaplains. Having a strong religious background, Katie Beth gravitated towards those working in the base chapel, it seemed natural. She felt at home in the religious setting and with the people who worked there. She and her husband had often attended Protestant Chapel services at several bases where they lived.

Once stationed at Fort Greeley, Alaska, it became common for the Catholic Chaplain, Father Andrew to stop by to visit Katie Beth in her home. He often made trips to other military installations and upon returning would deliver magazines and newspapers for her to read. As much as she appreciated his thoughtfulness and generosity, it struck Katie Beth funny to think that a priest was bringing her literature representing such a different faith than his own. Katie Beth imagined her strict religious parents would be shocked at such a gesture. Katie Beth took it in stride and was grateful for the inclusiveness of this man's undiscriminating faith. It persuaded her to become more open to the priest and his religious ideals.

Katie Beth was a runner. When her children were young, she would get up in the early hours of the morning and run before Peter went to work. At Fort Greeley, they lived in a government-owned townhouse. Three townhouse buildings faced each other making a U-shape. Inside the U was a driveway and parking spaces with a playground area in the center. As Katie Beth cooled down after her run, walking around the driveway several times, she began to hear cat calls—an odd phenomenon in the military married housing. Every morning someone whistled as she made her routine cool-down. Flattered, yet puzzled, she wondered who would be whistling. Everyone who lived in the 15 townhouses was married except the priest. It took some time before she identified that, yes, it was the priest who was whistling at her. A priest whistling at a married lady! This came as a bit of a shock to a naïve young woman, but she came to realize that sometimes the man cannot be taken out of the priest.

Katie Beth's education in priestly virtues expanded with the move to an air base in the Midwest where she lived across the street from Father Ted. This chaplain wasn't as shy as Father Andrew. Rather, Father Ted had a bigger than life personality and everyone loved him. The back of Ted's house faced the front of Katie Beth's, so she often saw his comings and goings as his car sat outside his back door when he was home. Katie Beth and Ted became fast friends, discussing theological and social issues. He often enjoyed just sitting out with Katie Beth and Peter on beautiful evenings.

While living there, Katie Beth held the position of Youth Director at her local church off base. She and Father Ted would discuss her activities with her youth and his work with the Catholic teens on base at the chapel. They even collaborated on an overnight retreat for their youth charges. A reciprocal bond was developed as Father Ted began to seek out Katie Beth to unwind after tragedy struck the base. Katie Beth's husband Peter could find Father Ted in their living room at all hours being consoled or assured by his wife.

One sunny afternoon, while Peter and Katie Beth were outside working on the garden in their front yard, Peter suggested Katie Beth go across the street to invite Father Ted to go out on their boat on the nearby lake for dinner later in the week. Katie Beth innocently trotted across the street past Father Ted's car up to the back door. She could hear music playing loudly, but there was no answer to her knock. Since Father Ted was known to work in his front garden, she walked around to the other side of the house to see if she could find him. There was no evidence of Ted working in the garden, so she mounted the steps onto the sprawling front porch. The door was open with only a screen door separating her from the inside of the house. She rang the doorbell and then looked up. To her surprise she saw at the top of the stairs in the bathroom a naked priest. Father Ted had just gotten out of the shower and was standing in what he thought was the privacy of his own home. However, an unexpected guest rang the doorbell. It was an awkward moment, indeed! Katie Beth felt the heat of blushing and quickly looked down as Father Ted spoke, "Who is it?"

"It's Katie Beth," she answered quickly. "Please come visit Peter and me when you have a chance."

Katie Beth was off that porch in a flash, returning to the safety of her husband and his confidence. Shortly after returning to her own yard, Father Ted casually sauntered over with his head bowed, not making direct eye contact. Katie Beth and Peter greeted Father Ted as if nothing had happened. They enjoyed a pleasant visit on the porch. Nothing was said about the naked priest—nothing, ever. The three continued to enjoy their evenings especially on the boat for dinner cruises.

Not long after the shocking naked priest event, Katie Beth heard that Father Ted was being transferred overseas. The Catholic Chapel congregation was putting on a farewell dinner in Father Ted's honor. It was going to be a surprise "roasting" for the Father. After all, he was a bigger-than-life man—who could dish out the humor. Now, it would be the community's chance to serve it back to him. He had no idea what was on the dinner menu for entertainment until he arrived that night.

Since it was well known around the community that the Clarks were friends with the Father, Katie Beth was to be the token Protestant "roaster." Everyone anticipated that she had lots of goods to tell about her friend. This put Katie Beth in a moral dilemma that she literally had to pray about. What was she going to say? She was so concerned about betraying the friendship she had with Father Ted, but it was true she had some "dirt" on him. How far should she go?

The evening of the dinner arrived. As Katie Beth started up the steps of the Officer's Club, she saw Father Ted on the porch anxiously waiting with program in hand.

When their eyes met he said, "Are you really going to roast me?"

Seeing how intent and worried he was, Katie Beth laughed and said, "Well, they asked me, and I couldn't resist honoring their request to celebrate you, Ted." He didn't appear any too relieved. With that, they both went to their seats.

Peter and Katie Beth were sitting quite far apart from the guest of honor's table. In fact, the Officer's Club was so crowded for this farewell dinner, when it was Katie Beth's turn to speak, she had to walk out into the hallway, travel down the hall, and go back into the ballroom to get to the podium. Katie Beth could hear over the sound system that people were chuckling as Father Ted uttered words she couldn't quite make out. It was evident by the way he wiped his brow that he was nervous about what she was about to say.

Katie Beth reached the podium. She looked out over the crowd, thinking how much love was in that room for this man that had shepherded them for years. She looked at Ted, smiled, and began:

"Oh, how I love Father Ted, let me count the ways...."

There were many things Katie Beth could count in the ways Father Ted had made a difference in her life, the life of her family, and those in the community. It was fun to recount each one as she went through them, one by one. When she was done, Father Ted responded sincerely with a "Thank you," that held more gratitude than anyone in the audience could know. Katie Beth and Father Ted knew that their unspoken secret would remain intact and they both felt peaceful relief.

Many people touched and enriched Katie Beth as she journeyed through her military life experience. Her exposure to new friends of different faiths, especially two Roman Catholic priests, allowed her to broaden her horizons and develop a deeper understanding, tolerance and love for those with different worldviews than her sheltered upbringing had equipped her for life's journey.

SEASONS

Nancy Damon Burke

First rays of sunshine
Break night into dawn
April leaves quietly
May carries on.

In the peace of the garden
A quiet is found
Birds chirp their greetings
A symphony of sound.

A brilliant male cardinal
Calls piercing the din
To entice a shy female
He's seeking to win.

Warmth of the sun
Lift bulbs in the ground
Poking their sprouts
Through the soil with no sound.

Soon to make beautiful
Their own patch of earth
Each petal and blossom
A sign of rebirth.

Winter is waning
Though yearning to stay

Spring has proved stronger
With each passing day.

Summer sun rises early
Scorching the land.
Crops bursting the harvest
Their bounty so grand.

Fields turn to amber
Their duty is done
Days grow still shorter
Fall now has won.

Chilled air blows softly
Leaves turn bright then fall
Too soon a white blanket
Covers it all.

Seasons are witness
To all that we know.
Sunrise in morning
Sunset's last glow.

We pass through this world
We ramble and roam
Till The Lord offers his hand
And says, "Come now, you're home."

THE FOG HAS RISEN

Joanne McIntosh-Davidson

Mindful meditations can become more strenuous than climbing a mountain: sometimes even more tiring and stressful. Then again, they can be like a slippery slope to disaster or a fresh breath taking in views of success and happiness.

I attended a writer's workshop at Bascom Lodge on the top of Mount Greylock in North Adams, Massachusetts. It was touted as a restful inspirational workshop with magnificent views. The clouds and fog had rolled in for hours. Condensation smeared the windows to create a shield. We could only make out the shapes of the top of the trees. We were encouraged to use our imaginations as to what the serene scenic view looked like beyond the foggy overcast.

The meditation portion of the workshop turned out to be an inspiring time. Many began writing about the views, the fog rolling in covering the wooded background, and vacations that had been transformed into new adventures by the weather. I joined those looking inward to their souls, as I did.

The inner voice can produce a heavy thick fog. It can congeal your thoughts and words into negative messages that destroy your faith, your belief in yourself, and might even force you to suicidal thoughts and actions. Yet again, that same inner voice can lead you on an inspiring journey and bring excitement and success. I chose to peer through the fog in search of my true essence. In doing this I had to face some very dense fog.

You can lose your confidence and self-esteem by meditating on the negative thoughts and words of others: beginning to believe these words as they become so many and so real. They eventually appear to be large mountains difficult to go through, around, over, or even to dig under. They destroy your soul and convictions.

I had allowed the cruel, negative words of an acquaintance, whom I also considered to be a friend, to destroy me. With numerous injuries and a serious heart attack caused by this undue stress, I became stuck in the fog and muck of my mind. I lost my self-confidence, my belief in me and the belief that I can be successful again.

I turned to the Lord in prayer so many times to help me, but I needed to be quiet enough to listen for His words of encouragement.

One morning, not long after the workshop, as I sat with my Bible on the table in front of me, I randomly opened it and turned immediately to a section in 1 Peter 5:6. "Therefore, humble yourselves under the mighty hand of God, that He may exalt you in due time, casting all your care upon Him, for He cares for you."

In 2 Peter 1:5-7, Apostle Peter mentions the qualities that I needed to improve my confidence and focus on my strengths and abilities. He mentioned faith, virtue, knowledge, self-control, perseverance, godliness, kindness, and love. Those qualities that will help me to reach my goals in life. God has given me everything that I need.

I realized that I must let go of the resentment that I had harbored toward my so-called friend. I have been dwelling on her negative words, the words that were destroying me. As I turned toward my Lord, I began to think of His majesty, *He is in me and I in Him.*

My faith in my Lord grew as did my faith in myself. I began to regain my confidence and perseverance. My tenacity became stronger with each passing day. I also reached out to my family and friends for strength and reassurance. I began to feel and to receive their love and godliness that I was yearning for.

I wish for you, my friends, that your fog will begin to lift from your lives and that you will be able to see clearly how much you have to offer the world.

I am able to see clearly now that I am a capable and powerful woman who has so many talents and gifts to offer to others. The fog and negativity have lifted, and the confidence and belief that I can be successful again is shining through me, just like the sun shone through as the fog rose at the top of Mount Greylock.

A RETRO TALE

Sally Sennott

CAST

Sadie

Linda

Waiter

Young Linda

Rob

The current action takes place in and around a pub in 2018; and the fifties era flashback happens in the interior of a ranch house in small town America.

SCENE ONE--PRESENT DAY

The Red Cardinal Pub is not very busy and the waiter is attentive. SADIE and LINDA are ordering 'bites' of food. They are discussing the subject of the day, sexual harassment, over a leisurely midweek lunch.

Left stage is arranged as the interior of a pub. The back wall is brick and the square tables are covered with white tablecloths. As the curtain rises, LINDA and SADIE are seated front stage. The waiter is hovering nearby. He approaches the table. The women are in their mid-seventies with grey/white hair. Stylishly dressed in pants, they are engaged in conversation as the lights come up.

LINDA: Do you think things will ever change? I'm talking sexual harassment. You know it's the subject of the times.

SADIE: They're changing now. Men in politics and the board room—in the movie industry and on radio—are being outed over their sexual antics.

LINDA: Even Bill Cosby is going through multiple trials.

SADIE: I saw on CNN just today, the FBI is raiding the office of Michael Cohen, President Trump's lawyer and fixer.

LINDA: You must remember Rob Franklin from high school? Rob was about five feet ten, had a crew-cut and exploring hands. He liked the chase.

SADIE: Yes, I *do* remember Rob. I went out with him for a while.

LINDA: Me, too.

SADIE, (*pausing between each word*): I—didn't—know—that!

LINDA: I never told you; but I learned a life lesson while seeing him.

SADIE: So today you come out to me about your relationship with Rob more than 60 years later? Why?

LINDA: You'll soon see the relevance.

SADIE: Okay, I'll take your word for it.

The male waiter approaches and collects the menus. He pours water from an iced pitcher.

WAITER: Good afternoon. Are you ready to order?

SADIE: The appetizer menu is perfect for us. I checked it out online. I don't want to overeat. (*SADIE glances at LINDA*) Let's share the grilled chicken and have the brussels sprouts again. Last time it was so good.

LINDA: (*looking across the table and then at the waiter*): And bring some eggplant and two plates. We'll share the 'bites.' And I'll have a glass of Sam Adams.

SADIE, (*to the waiter*): Chardonnay for me.

WAITER: Coming right up. I'll be right back with the drinks.

SADIE, *(resuming the conversation)*: Rob was sexually aggressive, as I remember. You had to fight his unwanted advances off with both hands. He had octopus arms.

They nod in agreement.

LINDA: Don't I know that! Sexual misconduct wasn't even a concept when we were growing up in the fifties. Now everyone's talking about it.

SADIE: We were groping in the dark, literally and figuratively, weren't we? (Pause). Yeah, I remember Rob. He was defined by his red sports car. It had the liquid lines of an exotic ride. He was back in high school after a stint in the service. I guess he didn't graduate with his class.

LINDA: That's right. And we were freshmen in high school and we were taking Algebra 1. As a returning student, Rob needed the credit to earn a high school diploma. What was he working towards? Becoming a state trooper?

The waiter returns, and they pause.

WAITER: Sam Adams and chardonnay. Enjoy. *(the women politely thank him; he exits)*

LINDA: *(after a beat)* Look, *(with emphasis)* I don't want you to think I was stealing your boyfriend. Still, I was concerned by the perceived embarrassment of being in the spotlight, so I didn't mention dating Rob at the time. And it was a rather...uncomfortable breakup to say the least...*(she trails off, not quite ready to take this trip down memory lane.)*

LINDA takes a sip of beer and leans back in her chair. It is dark in the pub and the chill envelopes her. She reaches for her fleece jacket which hangs on the back of her chair and pulls it over her shoulders, falling into a reverie. LINDA proceeds to put into words her impressions of Rob when a young teenager more than 60 years ago. She begins to reminisce. SADIE leans forward in her chair, riveted by the revelation at hand.

LINDA: Do you remember the clothing style that we used to wear? It was a time of poodle skirts and bobby sox. There was an air of innocence. The new thing was white bucks.

SADIE: How fashion has changed since then. Scarab bracelets were big, worn with tweed skirts and button-down shirts under crewneck sweaters.

LINDA: We were all trying to look like girls at an ivy league college, weren't we?

SADIE: In junior high I had started wearing bright red lipstick—no mascara or eyeliner. My chest had filled out.

SADIE smiles and takes a sip of wine. LINDA, looks across the table, and notices that SADIE is unconsciously sitting up very straight, which emphasizes her bustline.

LINDA: Yeah, I had big breasts, too. Rob was attracted to girls with big boobs, wasn't he?

SADIE: I was attracted to his car. It was a little red sports car and the top came down—it stood out. It was a shiny new convertible. There were only three student-owned cars in the high school parking lot. The car sure made an impression on me; the man, not so much.

LINDA: It sure did.

SADIE: I only went out with Rob about five times. All he was after was sex. We would go parking and his hands would be all over me. You had to fight him off. There was no verbal come on… He would cover my lips with his, and his hands would start moving rhythmically to the tempo of whatever song was on the radio. He was not a conversationalist and there was only one thing on his mind. I assume he thought he was like Trump or some other executive type, brash and aggressive. All about the action. He operated in overdrive.

LINDA: Our talk is really bringing me back to the time before men were held accountable for their sexual misconduct—rape, yes, but back then bad behaviour was brushed off as boys will be boys. (*She pauses, sips her drink.*)

SADIE: The girl's sexual history was always brought up, wasn't it! (*She shakes her finger in the air.*) For that reason, no one wanted to be an easy mark. One's reputation as a 'good girl' was very important in small town America in the fifties. Now the world is so much more sophisticated with television talk shows and the Internet. Victoria's

Secret ads are on TV. In our day, I remember the guys drooling over the bare breasts in National Geographic and whispering the name Hugh Hefner in hushed and reverent tones.

SADIE and LINDA chuckle together. SADIE sets her glass of wine on the table. She is on a conversational roll and gestures with both hands as she continues her diatribe.

SADIE *(continuing)*: Just take cable news broadcasters of today. If you want to be one you have to show cleavage and be able to banter with the male anchor. You wouldn't dare to appear on TV without false eyelashes and a professionally styled mane of long hair. *(SADIE looks directly into LINDA'S eyes.)* Tell me again why you didn't mention you were dating Rob at the time it was happening, IRL (in real life) as they say now?

LINDA: I didn't know how you'd take it. Boys used to have serial girlfriends. I was Rob's fancy. After you, anyway. Actually, I was affected by the embarrassment of being in the spotlight. *(She pauses.)* So, today I'm bringing it up.

Stage lights dim. An air of nostalgia descends on the stage as LINDA recounts life decades earlier.

LINDA *(continues)*: I remember the spring Rob and I were dating. It was 1956. I was fourteen - turning 15 in July. I had been wearing lipstick for two years. It was my first foray into car dating and I was impressed by Rob's vehicle – that little red sport convertible with the stick shift. We would go parking at the cemetery, or the sandbanks off John Fitch Highway. Sometimes after dark we would go to the drive-in movie. *(With emphasis)* It was before the sexual revolution. That happened in 1963 and was known as 'the pill!'

SADIE: Bingo! Thank God for the pill!

LINDA and SADIE both reach across the table and clink their drink glasses.

SADIE and LINDA, *(in unison)*: To the sexual revolution!

LINDA: Anyway, I felt grown-up and liked that I was playing in a new arena. I saw the adult world through the lens of my own experience. It was the best way to learn the twists and turns of the fast lane. *(Opening her mouth and drawing in air, gasping, and waving her right hand in excitement.)* I was sexually precocious! Couldn't wait to start dating! I had outgrown spin the bottle!

They both laugh hysterically.

SCENE TWO – FLASHBACK

The lights come up on center stage illuminating a couch placed horizontal to the audience. The setting represents the living room of a small ranch house. YOUNG LINDA and ROB briskly enter from stage right. They are laughing and holding hands. Rob sits down on the couch to YOUNG LINDA's right and leans back on the pillows, pulling YOUNG LINDA down. ROB leans sideways pushing YOUNG LINDA into a horizontal position. They begin making-out. YOUNG LINDA is wearing a brown cardigan and pleated skirt. Her hair is done up in a French twist. She is a tall, buxom girl, even in her flats. ROB is dressed in penny loafers, khakis, and a blue button-down shirt.

LINDA narrates, sitting in a director's chair which is positioned stage left. She starts talking in the shadow of the spotlight. There is the sound of a car pulling up as LINDA starts her monologue.

LINDA: After turning into the driveway and cutting the engine, Rob invited me into his house. He sat on the living room couch and pulled me down next to him. We started making out. He was feeling me up through my sweater. His octopus hands were caressing my breasts.

YOUNG LINDA: Where's your mother?

ROB: Work.

YOUNG LINDA: My mother's a stay-at-home mom. It's exciting to be alone with you here in the living room.

ROB: Hmm. Can you see the car out the picture window?

YOUNG LINDA: Yes, it's right there in the driveway.

LINDA, *(thinking out loud)*: How many times have we gone parking in that low-slung vehicle—and I was always protected by the gear shift that divided the leather seats.

ROB, *(rising unexpectedly)*: Come on. Let's take a shower together. We've got the whole house to ourselves. My mom's not home. Let's take advantage of it.

LINDA, *(narrating)*: I stood up uncertainly. We were standing there by the living room couch. I could feel his hand slip way down below the crack.

The couple act LINDA's narration as she delivers it.

YOUNG LINDA, *(straightforwardly)*: I don't know if I want to. I've got my period.

The couple continues to act out the narration in slow motion.

LINDA, *(narrating)*: He lifted the front of my skirt and touched me again.

YOUNG LINDA crosses her hands in front of her skirt to prevent ROB from violating her again.

ROB: No, you're not on the rag.

YOUNG LINDA, *(sarcastically)*: Have you ever heard of a tampon?

ROB, *(undeterred)*: Are you jailbait?

YOUNG LINDA, *(stammering)*: I, I think that I might be.

ROB steers YOUNG LINDA into the bedroom, anyway. YOUNG LINDA pivots, walking backwards through the doorway. ROB is guiding her, kissing her as they slow dance. The spotlight comes up on the bed simulating sunlight. It is a double bed and there is a tall bureau with a radio. ROB turns it on. "Love Me Tender" plays softly. ROB holds YOUNG LINDA closer. He pulls down the window shade and turns back to YOUNG LINDA. The lights go down. The moment of reckoning has arrived. Will LINDA accept the intended outcome as certain?

ROB, *(simply)*: Let's lie down on the bed.

YOUNG LINDA sits down on the bed, fidgeting with her hands. She crosses her arms. ROB joins her on the bed and puts his arm around her back. He massages her neck. He starts to ease her into a prone position.

ROB: Relax, girl. I don't bite.

YOUNG LINDA: I know. It's just that I've never made out in a bed before.

ROB: Lean back. Rest your head. These are real feather pillows.

YOUNG LINDA: These pillows really are nice. You sink right into them.

ROB: Why don't you let down your hair? You have pretty hair.

YOUNG LINDA: All right.

LINDA, *(narrating)*: My long hair framed my face and Rob played with it absentmindedly. I remember relaxing. Rob slipped off my flats and they dropped to the floor.

The couple act this out.

ROB: Honey, let's cuddle up. I really like you. Do you like me?

YOUNG LINDA: I do.

ROB aggressively climbs on top of Linda. Things turn eerie and dark.

LINDA *(narrating)*: He was unbuttoning my sweater and trying to unsnap my bra at the same time. It was a white cotton bra and I didn't wear my white nylon camisole that day. His intentions were undeniable. Rob was in overdrive.

ROB: Your skin's as soft as those feather pillows: Touch me, Linda. I want you so bad.

ROB guides YOUNG LINDA'S hand to his crotch.

ROB *(continuing)*: Pleasure me, baby!

The lights go down.

YOUNG LINDA: I can't.

The lights go out completely; pause. A panicky LINDA screams NO! Pause. A single light shines on Linda who has leaped off the bed to stop the encounter in the dark.

LINDA *(narrating)*: The hair on my arms stood up. I rose and apprehensively looked about. Rob moved to close the bedroom door.

The darkness enveloped us. I've made a terrible mistake, I thought. I've lost control of the situation.

Light comes on brightly now. YOUNG LINDA, *(has moved across the room away from Rob. She is clutching herself in shame)*: Let's go. I want to go, now. Take me home.

Rob stands near the door; he hesitates to shut it, he begins to pull it closed. Young Linda looks afraid. He stops.

YOUNG LINDA takes this as her opportunity to exit. Rob, mistaking this for her wanting him, grabs her hand and pulls YOUNG LINDA toward him. "You Ain't Nothing But a Hound Dog," begins on the radio.

YOUNG LINDA *(continues, insisting):* Didn't you hear me. Look, I know what you expect. I'm not ready to lose my virginity. Take me home, Rob!

She grows in confidence, knowing she has something he wants, but she won't give it to him.

ROB: Linda, take it easy! You're overreacting.

ROB pats YOUNG LINDA on the ass. He tries to kiss her again. She pulls away and forcefully pushes past him on her way to the living room.

LINDA, *(locking eyes with him she realizes he could be just as forceful and she loses her edge on the word home)*: Take. Me. Home.

ROB, *(somewhat seeing the error of his ways):* So, so... so, very sorry. *(shaking his head, defeated).* Sure, I'll take you home.

ROB and LINDA exit. Elvis trails off. "...cryin' all the time."

The couple exit stage right and the lights swing to stage left. SADIE and LINDA resume their conversation at the table in the pub.

SCENE THREE – PRESENT

As the lights fade on the bedroom, the lights rise on the pub scene. SADIE motions the waiter to refill the water glasses. LINDA daintily wipes her mouth with a cloth napkin. She reapplies lipstick using a compact mirror. LINDA and SADIE reconnect.

LINDA: Rob was a man, not a boy. I've put his unwanted advances behind me. Rob passed algebra and completed his programs. I don't know if he was sorry for what he did or sorry he didn't sleep with me. We stopped talking after that. And he went onto easier conquests. *LINDA blots her lipstick using a Kleenex and dabs at her eyes.)*

SADIE: Well, I heard he was up on sexual misconduct charges. Do you really think he stopped teenage girls just to proposition them? *You* were fourteen...guess he likes them young.

LINDA: It seems so obvious, but were we both just stupid kids? Did I know what I was doing? But I couldn't have known. What did I know? He definitely took advantage of my innocence. But part of me feels ashamed even while being the victim.

SADIE: Isn't that what this boils down to? They're all saying it happened to "me too." This is the movement. Victim or not I think we ladies ought to stick together. *She lifts her glass and Linda hesitates before joining her; still feeling shame.*

LINDA: I still struggle with it. It was such a close call. Him intent on taking what I didn't want to give. I always wanted to tell you, but I was afraid you'd call me a slut or worse.

SADIE: What's worse than slut? (she laughs)

LINDA: I don't know. *(LINDA isn't laughing and SADIE realizes she can't cut the tension with a joke and guiltily looks down.)* I'm just glad I could finally confide in you.

SADIE: *(pause; Sadie looks up; Linda reaches for her hand; Sadie takes it).* Me, too. I'm sorry you couldn't confide in me. The way I see it Rob was a man and you were 14. *You* were being propositioned. Back then there was no punishment for bad behavior... *(SADIE'S voice trails off, then comes back strong.)* In broad daylight he propositioned you. He had seven years on you, Linda. That's on him. Not *you.*

LINDA: He treated me like a piece of meat.

SADIE: Yes, but he didn't get a piece of ass, did he?

LINDA: No, he didn't. *(she finally cracks a smile, briefly)* It's a good thing I had my wits about me.

SADIE: 'Good thing' is an understatement.

LINDA: Now if you want me to be frank, (*shaking off the past with a sip of her drink and shake of her head*) my sexual initiation happened in a matchbox house, a 'ticky-tacky' house in the Whalom District. I got *myself* into that situation. My parents had no idea it happened. I didn't tell anyone, not even you. I was concerned about the fallout.

SADIE: That was always a fast part of town—not far from the lakefront and the allure of the Amusement Park. It seems like all girls becoming women are subject to these obscene advances. Love didn't enter into the picture.

LINDA: Yeah, I don't know. The difference was feeling like I had power then. The sex was on my terms even if I didn't care about the guy.

SADIE: But you were in a stressful situation.

LINDA: Yeah. I didn't know if he was really going to take me home. Was he going to push his luck? Was I in a safe place? I was scared.

SADIE: Point taken. Were we sluts, Linda?

LINDA: I think what you mean, were we the Madonnas or the whores…*(pause)* Let's go home.

LINDA and SADIE get up from the table and walk over to the shade of a tree in the parking lot. The lights rise imitating the natural light of day.

LINDA (*continuing*): Thanks for coming out today. I had no idea it would turn into a therapy session. Now I'm starting to feel bad again.

SADIE: We've got to stop feeling sorry for ourselves. Sometimes I think we're all too Puritan for our own good. We can't talk about sex without it being awkward or dangerous. And yet, we both agree it's the best feeling in the world! *LINDA AND SADIE laugh together, join hands, and walk toward stage right.* You were only a girl. He weren't nothing but a hound dog was he?

SADIE and LINDA embrace in the parking lot. They spontaneously dance and begin singing, "You ain't nothin' but a hound dog."

LINDA: *HE* ain't ever caught a rabbit…

SADIE: And *HE* ain't no friend of mine.

They laugh and exit with arms draped over each other's shoulders; the laughter fades as the light goes to black.

CURTAIN

CHIRPING

Steven Michaels

A lone chirp
can be silenced
by the stomping of one's heel.
How easy it is to squelch
individuality
with an authoritative boot.

But the lone soldier
will reignite
the call
once it senses the all-clear
little wondering
if the threat can still hear it.

So should we all.
Call out
to our silenced brethren
to ignite
the harmonious stirrings
of hope
among the lowly
the alone
and us all.

PROFILES

James Thibeault

It was the way that Ajay did nothing that made him so attractive to Claire. While most of the high school students in first lunch sat with friends and stared at their phones, Ajay stared up at the ceiling tiles.

He methodically ate his apple while his head arched all the way back. Although his clothing was baggy Claire gazed at the tight, corded muscles around his neck. He was strong but hid it well. Claire fantasized he was some sort of Clark Kent—once he ripped off the shirt, power roared from his veins. She typically didn't go for overtly strong men, but his containment was too irresistible to ignore. On top of that, Claire also found the ceiling tiles fascinating. They were those ceiling grids with thousands of holes—punctured by decades of pencils and pens. In fact, there were still a few writing utensils lodged above. Perhaps he, too, marveled at the forgotten history. But she didn't know enough about him to be certain. His circle of friends didn't Venn diagram Claire's circle of friends—thus there lacked any link between them so far.

"Hey!" Mary waved a hand over Claire's glazed stare. "I thought we were going to leave a few minutes early, so we can study for Spanish."

"What? Oh, okay."

"Are you still staring at him?"

"Yeah, I think I'm going to talk to him." Claire felt her legs tremble, but she couldn't contain her excitement. She brushed back her hair and smiled. Before she stood up, Mary sat her back down.

"Woah, easy killer," said Mary. "You don't know anything about this guy, so how do we know he's not some crazy serial killer?"

"Does he look it?" Mary and Claire continued watching Ajay. He threw his half-eaten apple in the trash without averting his eyes from the ceiling. "Alright, so he's got the coordination, but why the hell is he staring at the ceiling so much?"

"I do it from time to time."

"You know what's he's thinking? He's thinking the best way to hide a body up there when no one is looking." Mary tried again to divert Claire's attention. "Think about it, it smells constantly like spoiled milk up in here, so no one will notice the rotting corpse."

"You're being a little paranoid, you think?"

"Nah, I'm not. You don't hit on people you don't know. Even dogs sniff around before they do the deed."

"Mary, I just want to talk to him."

"No, you don't. As your friend, I need to make sure you are safe. What if this guy gets overly attached to you and starts following you around everywhere? Sending you texts at 3 a.m.—talking how much of a 'nice guy' he is."

Claire sighed—he *was* staring at the ceiling tiles for a bit too long.

"Okay, so what do I do?"

"Recon. I'll get everything you need to know on him. What's his last name?"

"I don't know."

"Seriously? That doesn't help. You know how many Ajay's are out there?"

"Well, then what?"

"Here." Mary reached into her backpack and pulled out a notebook. "Go over there and say that you're doing a petition."

"For what?"

"You're smart. You're on the Dean's list, figure it out."

Claire let out a groan, chugged the last of her soda, and hastily grabbed the notebook.

As she approached him, she held the notebook tight to her chest. Ajay had a 5 o'clock shadow, and it was hard to tell if he did that deliberately or if he forgot to shave. It didn't matter, he looked damn good with it. His hazel eyes were soft, as he continued to focus sharply on the ceiling. Maybe this was a mistake, she thought. Maybe he had already put a body up there, and he was admiring his handicraft. Claire turned around, but Mary waved her hands back toward Ajay's direction. Claire mouthed, "No" violently. Mary mouthed something back that Claire couldn't understand. Before Claire walked back to her seat, she took one last look at Ajay. That was when Mary shouted, "Hey, Ajay." Ajay snapped out of his meditation and looked around. Eventually, he locked eyes with Claire and she instantly blushed. Damnit, she thought, just say something!

"Hello…"

"Hi."

"You're Ajay, right?"

He smirked. "Yes, that's me."

"Okay." Claire wanted to run right there but held her ground. She didn't speak for what seemed like eternity.

"Can I help you?"

"Yes!" she said suddenly. "Yes, you can absolutely help me." Claire spoke rapidly. "I am going around and asking people to sign a petition for … the … ceiling to be … historically … preserved. You know how they preserve things, like, strawberries. Well, it wouldn't be anything like strawberries, but a ceiling … and it wouldn't be in a jar."

Ajay laughed, soft and deep. Claire was falling for him hard, but she had to keep her cool. Otherwise, Ajay might lock her in the basement with his collection of other unsuspected teenagers—as Mary had conjectured.

"You're funny," he said.

"Well, it's a serious issue…and I need your last name."

"Would you like my number, too?" Claire felt her toes tingle, but she bit her lip to ward off the excitement and realized that her front teeth were sticking out. Great, she thought, I'm definitely going to win him over now.

"Yes, all of your personal information. I'm mean … I'm not going to sell it or something—unless you got something juicy." Claire laughed nervously and turned to Mary, whose face was steeped in confusion.

"Just my last name, right? Miss CIA?" said Ajay.

"No, my name is … oh, you're funny … because … government." Her legs were beginning to lose the war against gravity. Claire began to shuffle her feet. What was wrong with her? Oh, she was blowing this. "Last name, please," Claire blurted out.

"It's Kohli, Ajay Kohli."

Suddenly, Claire laughed. She spoke loudly to get Mary's attention.

"Oh! Kohli! What an interesting last name. Is that Spanish?"

"Uh, no. It's Hindu. My parents were from Mumbai."

"Really? When did you come to the US?"

"When I was a kid, I don't really speak Hindi anymore. My mom still yells it though."

Claire didn't know if that was funny, but she laughed away. Ajay laughed too. Claire began to feel balanced again. Just do it, she thought, ask him out this weekend.

"Hey, I was wondering if you would—" Her phone buzzed, and she stared at the screen. Mary's face was front and center with a text below: RUN! Claire glanced over at Mary, who was continuing to type. Another message appeared: HIS PROFILE PICTURE IS JUST A SHOVEL!

Claire felt the blood draining away from her face. She couldn't breathe. "I have to go."

"What?"

"Bye."

She kept her head down and speed walked back to her table—not looking back at Ajay. Mary blew a sigh of relief.

"That was close."

"You're telling me. A shovel?"

"Yeah! I told you he was going to kill you."

"Is he looking at me?"

Mary looked in Ajay's direction. "Yeah."

Gently, Claire put the notebook to her face and turned to look at Ajay. She slowly lowered the notebook so that the tips of her eyes could glance at him. He stared at her like he did with the ceiling—those soft eyes had such strong emotions. She lifted the notebook and looked back at Mary.

"You see how he's staring at me?"

"He's probably thinking about which golf course to bury you in. I heard that there's a woman by the 10th hole, but the owner of the golf course refuses to do anything."

"What?" said Claire, a little surprised.

"Yeah, it happened like … a few years ago."

"Mary, did you just make that up?"

"No."

"Can I see that profile picture?"

"No, he's crazy. You saw how he stared at you. I'm not going to lose you."

"Give me your phone."

"No. Let's just go to Spanish already." Mary stood up and began to leave. Claire opened up her phone and looked at Ajay's profile. When Mary turned around, she tried to reach for Claire's phone. "*Vamonos!* Put the phone away!"

"Mary," Claire said softly. "It's a black and white photo."

"So?"

"It has a dog next to it."

"It's his attack dog!"

"*Dios mío.*"

Claire stood up and walked back to Ajay, who was back to looking at the ceiling.

"Why are you doing that?" Claire asked, sharply.

"Excuse me?" Ajay's voice was harsher, not as pleasant.

"Why are you staring at the ceiling?"

"No reason."

"Look," Claire pulled up a chair next to him. "I really like you. But if you are going to murder me, I would like to know now, so I can have a running head start."

Ajay looked around nervously. "I think I'm going to go to class."

"No please. I'm sorry. I'll make you a deal, if you tell me why you're staring at the ceiling—provided it doesn't freak me out—then I'll ask you out to a movie this Friday."

For a moment, Ajay looked at Claire.

"You serious?"

Claire blushed, "Yeah. So, we got a deal?"

Ajay paused again, his eyes slowly scanning Claire. He checked her out, but not sexually. It was more like profiling.

Claire's fingers drummed the table. What was taking him so long, she thought. He probably did bury that dog on the phone with his shovel.

"When I lived in Mumbai," Ajay said softly, a bit embarrassed, "I was so little, I don't remember anything. Apparently," he hesitated. "I used to stare at the apartment ceiling so much that my parents joked that I didn't need any toys." He smiled slyly. "It's the same pattern," he pointed towards the ceiling. "I thought if I kept looking at it—it could bring back some memories."

Claire burrowed her head into her shirt and groaned. Then she stared up at the ceiling.

"I'm an idiot."

"No, I get it. It's because…" Ajay gently rubbed one of his shoulders.

"Please, let's try this again." Claire stood up and walked all the way back to her table. Mary was still sitting there, perplexed.

"What happened?" she asked.

"A redo."

Claire walked back to Ajay, who was now standing up with his backpack. She took a deep breath and spoke.

"Hi, my name is Claire and I like how your neck does this weird tense thing ... um ... you are nice, and I would like to ..." She felt the blood rush to her face, but she continued. "... go to a movie together?"

"Yes," he smiled. Claire felt as if she melted into a puddle.

As they walked out of the cafeteria together, Claire asked, "You got a shovel, right? Would you bury someone at a golf course? Because I wouldn't."

"I think it's better than the ceiling. Why? Do you need me to do something?"

Claire stopped walking, then saw Ajay smirking. She smirked back and tapped him coquettishly on the arm.

LAST EXIT BEFORE THE TOLL

Steven Michaels

Mark hadn't realized his bouts of depression were getting worse—or he had and didn't care. After all, that's what depression feels like: not caring. Either way, his current condition had brought him here to the street corner where everything began unraveling. The only certainty he felt at this moment was a strong desire to wait outside a city apartment building, preparing to right a personal wrong.

• • •

In fifth grade, Mark remembered reading the *Phantom Tollbooth*. In his graduate studies, he often reflected on the book's profound literary strength and philosophical postulates which made it the postmodern *Wizard of Oz*. And despite the many fantastic adventures in which a boy named Milo stumbles into after driving a go-cart through a cardboard tollbooth into a land of enchantment and mathematics, the thing that stood out most to both Mark's younger self and collegiate soul was the book's foray into the Doldrums. And although Mark was uncertain as to the exact moment his depression started, this book had made it very clear that such a place did exist.

The book, apart from being an amusing fantasy, gave him solace to think that someone could venture to the land of the Doldrums and come out the other side. Moreover, Mark had been diagnosed not merely as depressed, but as manic-depressive. A name, which sometime around those college years, got changed to bipolar disorder by the medical profession.

In fact, Mark had always felt the term manic-depressive did him a disservice. That he should experience a "mania" as a result of being morose for weeks seemed insensitive to him. Mark never considered himself unhinged, and yet that was what the name implied. It also didn't help that people called him Manic-Mark behind his back. He had heard it rumored that he didn't get invited to parties because it was a gamble over who'd show up: Manic-Mark or his alter-ego, Mr. Melodramatic—the one who began weeping after one too many alcoholic beverages. Needless to say, Mark spent much of his high school years isolated from his peers.

College, despite what most people say, was not all that different. Somehow the cliques, the rumors, and all the other sludge of humanity followed him to those campuses of higher learning. And all the while, Mark kept going in and out a 'phantom tollbooth,' paying what seemed an increasing fee on the exit towards the Doldrums. He nearly failed out his Sophomore year, lost his scholarship, and had to get a job. Then, he lost the job due to erratic behavior and an incident with a co-worker; something Mark kept suppressing as it had been so uncharacteristic of him. Violent tendencies as a result of frustration, especially those that rendered another person unconscious due to a blow were not generally Mark's modus operandi. And yet...

Regardless of the one-time incident, Mark eventually managed to get his life back on track by bringing up his GPA through summer classes and calling a therapeutic call center and hanging up. Ironically, the disorder that had destroyed his social calendar had also afforded him the time to complete his studies. Somehow, the highs and lows of his polarity disorder coincided enough with fate to ensure that he never actually reached the proverbial rock bottom.

Until the court summons came.

Thus, despite Mark's best intentions to pretend it never happened, the co-worker seemed less willing to let the water pass beneath their mutual bridge. Meanwhile, as the incident lay in the dormancy of Mark's mind, it appeared as though time had been on his side, much like the faithful watchdog Milo encountered when his small automobile stalled out in the land of the Doldrums. Now, however, it seemed the watchdog had been merely keeping time, awaiting the day Mark's life would take a dark turn.

Much darker and grayer than the land of the Doldrums.

And so, Mark had been subpoenaed to appear in court to face a personal injury lawsuit filed by his former co-worker. Mark's lawyer did not seem overly concerned about the matter since Mark had no history of violence, and he assured Mark that one good character witness was all he needed to win the case against him. Indeed, the incident had occurred some time ago, and it seemed to be in Mark's favor that the victim had waited this long. Yes. It all came down to one good character witness—which would have been easy to get if Mark had had any friends.

So, naturally, Mark took a different approach.

A few days after meeting with his lawyer, Mark decided he would confront his former co-worker and convince him that it had all been one big misunderstanding; that picking up a small appliance like a blender and bashing it upside someone's head wasn't as serious as some people made it out to be.

And so, under the cover of darkness and unbeknownst to Mark's lawyer who would undoubtedly have said it was a bad idea, Mark now hid outside the apartment complex waiting for his old co-worker to come home. Thanks to social media, Mark had had no problem tracking down the address along with learning the person's arrival and departure times due to a lack of privacy settings.

While standing there in the dark, Mark pondered how others would assume his disorder led him to this life of stalking. But that's the trouble with so many people: they assume things. And to his knowledge, being bipolar was not a prerequisite for the role of stalker. In fact, Mark had never stalked someone before, and yet here he was: a bipolar man tracking what had recently become an obsession for him. And he realized this was the problem: his disorder had pigeon-holed him his whole life. This man standing in the dark, teetering on the brink of madness was not him.

Mark could very well have been diagnosed with split personality disorder because of the same emotional extremes inherent in his condition. But apart from some key differences, Mark couldn't be sure if he did suffer from having a split personality. The current situation did bring back the painful memory of those who called him either Manic Mark or Mr. Melodramatic, as predetermined by his mood, and his long suffering had often led him to wonder whether the real Mark existed at all.

Unfortunately, Mark had never gone to therapy with much regularity. In school, the powers that be recommended he see the school psychologist, but thanks to the depression, Mark could skip school and avoid this altogether. Meanwhile, it was becoming increasingly inevitable that any future therapy would be court mandated.

Just then, a familiar figure appeared at the end of the block where Mark now stood. It was Nigel. Mark barely remembered him, so it was too bad Nigel had so vehemently remembered him. Perhaps if Mark had given him a stronger blow to the head, the kind that could cause amnesia, none of this would be happening. And yet, how sad it was that this was Mark's only regret.

What had they even been arguing about that day? Why had Nigel waited so long to press charges? What could he possibly hope to gain after any lapse of time? It wasn't like Mark had continued to harass him; nor did he see him after being fired. In many ways, Mark had forgotten all about the incident. But not Nigel.

A few feet from the door, Nigel paused to take out his key. The moment for Mark to confront him had now arrived. But how would he do it? An apology followed by a plea for Nigel not to ruin his life by taking him to court? And wasn't Mark's life already in ruin thanks to his never-ending disorder?

I shouldn't be here, thought Mark as he stepped off the curb and crossed the street toward Nigel.

Then it occurred to Mark exactly why he *had* hit him all those years ago. It was the same reason he cringed whenever a certain actress came on the television. Despite a certain decency at her craft, there remained a quality about this person Mark did not like. And she, like Nigel, was simply unlikeable. Very unlikeable. And so, Mark, like some lone vigilante, felt it necessary to pummel Nigel, as if being unlikeable, as well as annoying, were the worst of crimes.

And as Mark crept closer to Nigel, he desperately wished for a stick or other blunt object, just as he had done before. He did detest himself for thinking this, but the urge to strike Nigel down became stronger with each step. And that he could later blame his behavior on his disorder was most reassuring, as he balled his fist in preparation for striking Nigel's offensive face.

Looking back, Mark would see this had nothing to do with his disorder. For in the moment, it was simply about Nigel and Mark, and Mark's hatred not for humanity, but quite literally, *this* fellow man. For Mark really did hate Nigel with every fiber of his being, regardless of his disorder. And yet, it also felt as though lashing out at Nigel would assuage the disorder, if only for the briefest of moments, just before the cops could haul him away.

So that is precisely what Mark did. Rather unsportsmanlike, too. For Mark took to striking Nigel from behind with not so much as a warning.

Nigel staggered and turned suddenly.

"What the—," he uttered as Mark released a powerful uppercut causing Nigel to fall to the pavement. And in that moment of watching Nigel collapse into a concussive state, Mark realized he didn't need to see his enemy bleed out to know he much hated him and himself.

For Nigel was never the problem. Only the victim. Only the last toll.

The 911 operator spoke in an even and well-trained tone; bereft of emotion as if anticipating a prank call or some other misuse of the emergency system. In a near similar tone, Mark informed the operator of what he had done, and there was a definite pause before the operator responded to him. She had heard of people calling in to report their crimes, but this was her first. And when she did speak, she said: "Okay, tell me your location."

To which Mark replied: "...the Doldrums."

THE TEN-FOOT-TALL MAN

Dennis F. King

The last time I saw him he was hunched over as he walked with small but steady steps. I was waiting for him to arrive at the Dunkin Donuts attached to the grocery store. The drive-thru window is busy non-stop in Spencer, since it is on Route 9, but the two-lane rural part of the Washington Highway. I was living in W. Brookfield in the Wickaboag Valley. There is a Donut Shoppe there, but it seemed to be mostly for two to four older women who enjoy having their weekly get-out (gab) place, but not for me. I tried going in at different times but never connected with anyone to just shoot the bull with. It was by accident that I stopped at that little one and saw the old man inside sitting there facing at the counter. He had an eye on everyone and almost everyone said, "hi Frank" and the young girls would hug him and say "Hi, Mr. Jones."

It was obvious he was a town favorite, but I did not know why. I decided to make friends with him. Sure, I enjoyed seeing all the pretty girls, the women running in and out of the place, because the drive-thru took longer. Most of the men had a nod for him, a wave of the hand and maybe a simple small-town question, "are you still around after all these years?" He looked healthy for his age in his early 80's.

He had a regular daily special of two trips a day at the same coffee shop and three times a week for lunch at the old-style Diner right around the corner. His blue older Chevy truck was always clean and in perfect condition, people know you by your vehicle in a small town, I found out later he had big trucks too. Another coffee drinker told me one day to come to the Parade next time and you will see Frank in it, waving to the crowds.

Those frequent visits there with Frank became light sessions of me hearing about his long, interesting life. He and I hit it off right away when I told him I was an Army Infantry veteran and he was too. I did not know I would become a writer at that time, but I loved biographies when I read books. I had read books on all the U.S. Presidents and had been in Berlin guarding the last Nazi leader. Frank liked that story from my life.

He stated that his military connection started just before World War II broke out. He wanted to join up but was still too young. There was a unit on Route 9 in Framingham, Massachusetts right at the intersection of Rt. 126 where he took the daily East-West Bus service. On a prior visit he had picked up an enlistment application and now he was back ready to join.

An Officer asked for his papers and after examining them noticed because he was not old enough, yet that Mother Jones had signed his permission to join. At this time Frank was a tall, strapping 6' 6" young man, raised on a farm and knew the importance of hard work. This helped, but the officer noted Mothers' signature looked like "chicken scratchin." He told him she could not write real well. He was accepted but kept it quiet at home for a while.

We talked about that first unit he was in and how because of his size and strength, a water-cooled machine gun was put in his arms. We both smiled because I also knew that machine gunners tend to be big, pack-mule type guys who have a hard-nose grin on their faces as they sweat all day. He told me they had assignments in Rhode Island coastline areas watching for enemy attacks and spies. This was all before the war broke out. Once it did, he said he went home, kissed Mother goodbye and said, "I am going to war."

I had a little homework for myself to clarify his story. I would go home at night and find a few pictures of machine gunners but foreign armies. I printed them out and would ask Frank the next time I saw him, "is that you with the water-cooled machine gun?" He used his good eye to look closely and said: "Nope, that's a Russkie Gunner." He was correct but I liked showing him things like military gear on Ebay for sale. Then there were the days when a local person might sit and talk about town happenings with Frank, so I just shut up and listened. It was a very hard thing for some of us to do. He was also very interested in my stories about my service and the assorted weapons I carried. It was a two-sided friendship.

One day he told me a story about how they were put on ships and after a long voyage they landed in Oran, a place I had never heard of. He told of troops gathering there for the ultimate attack and landing in Italy, still an Axis Power then under the Dictatorship of Benito Mussolini. Oran was located in North Africa where after Rommel and the Nazis were basically defeated there, our forces gathered for the Italian Campaign.

The day came when they boarded ships again and after landing and heavy fighting, a foothold was taken on the Italian Coast. That was a huge win, but the Nazis had fortifications and big guns to hold troops back. He told me they sat there for two months. No one knew why as the war raged everywhere. In military logistics a base is founded, then protected as the buildup of troops and supplies happen. He said they ate plenty of rations and not much else. It rained plenty, which made everyone wet and miserable with impassable roads. The planners think about that stuff, but guys like Frank, had to hurry-up-and-wait and were dependent on decisions from the higher ranks.

He told me, eventually our Army did move out and the fight was on as it began slowly since the terrain in Italy is part of the mountainous Alps. One day he told me that they fought their way into Rome and captured the City. The fighting had been very heavy. Frank said, as he was walking with his unit, a Medic came rushing over to him, looking him over asking, "Where are you hit?" And he replied, "I was not hit, but a Jewish guy from New York I knew was killed instantly; this is his blood on me." The Medic said he must put on a clean uniform immediately. They gave him one and he obliged for the morale of the troops.

For the next part of his story he was stationed in Germany, near a forest. He said he liked it there, and it reminded him of his home with all the trees and farmland. Being an old country boy, his early morning job was to split firewood for the cooks to use for breakfast, they knew he could swing an axe. He told me one day that the Germans split their wood later in the mornings, about 10AM, shaking his head at how lazy they were. One morning he could hear wood chopping off in the far distance, so he told his group to be silent as he used his ears while turning in a circle. He then picked up his machine gun and fired up over the trees towards the sound, he laughed because it stopped. They were that close to the enemy at times. The one thing I remember the most were his words that if they saw a Nazi with the SS emblem on their uniform or helmet that those soldiers were shot in the head, so as to be killed and not simply wounded. The look on his face was that of a man who had seen it, done it and knew why. It was fight or die. Finally, the war was over, and the troops came home. Frank came back to Spencer to start a new life.

I recall that he said he met a very beautiful French girl who worked in a mill nearby and before long they were married. I met his son once and I believe he has a daughter there too. I have forgotten what he did for work, but he was a Volunteer Fireman. He was a local boy, a W.A.S.P.- White Anglo Saxon Protestant but he married a French Roman Catholic girl so he was in the group of guys with "other than" wives. That area like much of Massachusetts and New England had a dozen large ethnic communities to work and live.

When Frank reminisced about his fireman days It seems impossible now, but he wondered out loud to me about how many fires could have been put out sooner. What really happened was that one team was on one side of the house shooting their hoses through the first-floor windows and it came out the windows spraying Franks' team of the "other than" volunteers. They had those "peeing contests" many times back long ago.

Now I was learning how everyone knew of him, a local, a WWII veteran and a fireman all his life. In the olden days you stayed in your town from cradle to grave and loved it, nothing else was better than home.

A month later I was visiting with a couple of guys, as I had my coffee and donut special, but no Frank. I asked if they had seen him. "Yes, they replied Gone to the Doctor with his son." We chatted about this small-town legend. I asked how well they knew him, and they replied, "all our lives. Our parents knew him, too." One guy asked if I had seen his trucks, two of them, pristine, rebuilt World War II Deuce and a Halfs. I never knew about them and Frank did not brag about those things. That day I learned about Frank always driving in the town parades. He and his son attended big military events to show them. That day I realized who he really was: a Ten-Foot Tall Man.

It took me a few visits to run into him again. And he was looking good, smiling, still wearing tan construction boots, Dickie pants, as well as being clean shaven donning a fresh haircut. He told me the Doctor had asked him how he felt, and Frank replied "I feel great for 84 years old" but the doctor shook his head from side-to-side and said, "NO, that can't be. Here is another pill." And that young doctor got a shock when Frank told HIM where he could take that pill because he sure as hell wasn't!

I called him the Ten-Foot-Tall Man once, and he smiled and asked why, since he was now hunched over at the waist and only about 5'6" now. I told him, "you were 6'6" the day you lied that Mother could not write, but you joined the Army, so I gave you an extra foot for that. Then you married that French girl, loved her to the end, despite the small-town discrimination and so you gained another foot for that. The fact that you continue to be the center of every parade in this town for 50 years to the delight of all, well, that counts too. Lastly, you keep our Military History with you always, so add another foot for that, and now you're 9'6. And naturally, I round up, so you are a Ten-Foot Tall Man."

He liked it and it made him smile proudly. Over the years, I've come to recognize Frank's caliber of man. I usually see them just sitting there minding their own business, and I am sure to nod, wave, and say hello while I still can. For there are a few other people I have encountered in life who have earned his same title: people who are simply, "bigger than life."

ODE TO JANET GUTHRIE

Steven Michaels

As she put it:
"Things were about to come unglued"

Her exploding engine
seemed imminent
as she raced the final laps

Pushing the gas pedal to the floor
knowing she'd be out of the race
not to mention the human one

Accelerating at top speed
she didn't realize she was breaking barriers
the first woman to qualify
for the Indy 500

There is something existential
in the way men race cars
No wonder it took a woman
to transcend the endless track

SUNDAY AT GRANDPA'S

Diane Kane

Sunday morning quiet

Open cans of tomatoes

Puree, chopped, and paste.

Only Contadina will do.

Garlic, oregano, palm full

of sugar. Mix. Check flame,

place cover askew.

Remove ground meat

from brown paper wrapper.

Brown eggs in yellow bowl

on table, room temperature.

Shake dew from freshly

picked parsley. Inhale.

Chop whimsy leaves. Mix

into breadcrumbs warm

from the oven. Kneed meat

with cracked eggs, pinch of salt,

Clove of garlic crushed

between blade of knife

and wooden cutting board.

Hand full of Parmesan

Cheese. Shh, secret ingredient.

Mix well. Inhale. Pull

handful of sticky mixture.

Roll until perfectly round.

Admire. Pour olive oil from

gold can into hot steel pan.

Place meaty orbs into

jumping grease. Turn, turn.

Pluck each ball from pan.

Plop into bubbling sauce.

Simmer all day. Steam drips

from windows. Sweet

smell permeates air

Taste buds dance.

Family arrives boisterous.

"Mangia, mangia!" Eat, eat!

Sunday Afternoon fulfilled.

THE ROAD, THE RIVER, AND THE HAIRPIN TURN

Dennis F. King

My favorite Massachusetts summer road trip starts at The French King Bridge heading west for the next sixty-five miles. It has been referred to as The Mohawk Trail for over one hundred years now to the tourists; I am one of them. There is something that happens to me as I meander up and down hills, gently steering my car. There are only two lanes here. It is either a long, mundane ride with the wife and kids moaning "are we there yet?" or all eyes, except the driver's, are glued to the windows.

In my opinion, it is best when the windows of the car are rolled down with the smells of a forest filling our lungs. Every country doctor will advise you to go and relax, whatever it takes and take several deep breaths. A city doctor may not give that advice considering bumper to bumper traffic and lungs full of exhaust fumes are not healthy and incite stress. It is probable that most tourists are taking many, many deep breaths noticing how good it makes them feel. The truth is that those who live on The Mohawk Trail in little villages still do not lock their doors or windows except for the barn and a gate.

Now in my later years, I seem to look more at the trees, and if the road runs alongside a river, my soul rests as I take it all in. This feeling of euphoria is so special to me because it does take me away and I like it and know when it is happening but only lately realized why it triggers good feeling in me. I know I like less traffic, plenty of tall trees and that water moving along beside me but now I have analyzed it. I never gave it any thought about the why or where it came from when a flashback happened to me recently, and it all became clear to me. It is amazing how our brains can hold information new and old without any effort, but then it happens.

My little brain showed me a movie that was in color whether my eyes were open or closed. It was about our yearly trip from Milford where we lived. The car was packed with my parents, my brothers Gary and Jamie up at 5 A.M., and the picnic basket full. We would get on Route 140 at the hospital and go west all the way to Route 122 just south of Worcester, then head north until we hit Route 2 and we headed west.

My family is part French, and Mom liked to stop on the famous bridge to stretch our legs. Dad had an unfiltered Pall Mall and the rest of us were figuring out where to pee. This bridge was built by the same company that built the George Washington Bridge in New York City and the most famous one of all, The Golden Gate Bridge in San Francisco.

The best part of the trip was when we pulled off the road on the riverside at a picnic table. They were plentiful back then and not a fast food joint anywhere in sight. I was the oldest boy and helped set up the table with a red and white checkered table cloth of *cloth* - no plastic ones yet. We always stopped at Mazzarrelli's Bakery for a fresh baked French stick. While the grinders were made, the other boys threw rocks into the water. Back then families had a big metal container with a wide top that unscrewed to fill it. Usually, homemade cold lemonade and when that was gone the Kool-Aide came out. There were other family travelers parked along the river just eating, resting and being part of Nature.

After a nice stop to fill up the gas tank, the trip began again heading west on Route 2 when something peculiar happened. Suddenly, we were heading north and then abruptly we came to the Hairpin Turn, a full U-turn on the top of a mountain. If your brakes failed, well, every kid knew what was next.

Back in those early 1960s, everyone stopped at the Gift Shop just before the turn. We were not a rich family, but we always came home with a Coonskin Cap and a Tomahawk. Mother insisted on a few pictures by the Giant Indian Statue on the trip.

We respected the area and the Indian Heritage. My young mind always imagined that bands of Indians had traveled over this ground we were on because it was true once. The whole atmosphere was being out in the woods, birds chirping and maybe see a skunk. Dad liked to remind us that Yogi Bear had relatives that live near this river. We kept our eyes peeled looking into those woods, especially when Dad cooked hot dogs. Even I knew that bears could smell food cooking, so I always asked for grinders, cold ones without the fire.

Those earliest of my memories are my strongest because of the trees, the water, light breezes moving the treetops. The scent of trees is everywhere, especially the evergreens and pines as well as the smell of the soil. My hometown was different. I lived in a three-family house and just down the street were several huge shoe shops where hundreds of folks worked every day doing piece work. There were plenty of sights and sounds and people everywhere when the work whistle blew twice a day.

I think that feeling as a young child riding in the family car - protected, provided for and loved by a family - is why now, as an old man, I can be moved to soulful rapture by a country road and its rolling mountains.

LAWN CARE

Steven Michaels

If I ask him why
it's so important to mow
every inch of field
and whack the weeds
which threaten the siding of the house,
he will say
because his father took great care of things.

He won't say
how spending months in Vietnam
has left him no choice but to beat back
all unyielding vegetation in his path.

The chaos jungle
has never left his mind.
Spring and Summer are painful reminders
that tall grass is the enemy,
its denseness
suffocating.

It's true
his father did create order in their yard.
He tries to live up to those expectations
but Agent Orange has limited his abilities
to stop the menace of leaves.

I feel his pain as I push the hand mower
up the steep backhill.
It doesn't compare to the hills
he marched on the way to Saigon,
save a near equivocal sense of
heat, sweat, redundancy
minus the insurmountable fear of death.

When I am done, I survey the land
cognizant there are no Charlies in my trees,
no wire fences to be mended
no thorns in my side
from a war before my time.

I loathe the task to be sure.
How easy it would be
to let the vegetation conquer the hill.
This is not my fight but his.
Had our lives been reversed
I probably would have dodged the draft.
Labelled a coward.
From the way he once worked,
it is clear he likes the battle.

Watching me,
he seems grateful,
for I try to be a good soldier
not asking any questions at all.

JOURNEY FROM THE VALLEY OF DEATH TO THE MOUNTAIN OF HOPE

Mary Louise Owen

There are times when the darkness of life seems so thick, that any light of hope fails to penetrate the barriers of discouragement, especially in the valley of death. May 2, 2002 began such a time for Sally.

One morning driving to work as a mental health therapist, Sally received a call beckoning her to a nearby high school for crisis intervention. One of the students committed suicide. Her skills were needed to help intervene with the student body's justified grief.

Sally and a team of crisis counselors went to work providing comforting care for the students and staff. She found it fascinating to watch God's grace in action as even students provided solace and healing for their other classmates. There was palpable evidence in the school that day, of a higher power among the grieving group. A light glimmered, penetrating and shining thru the darkness of grief—a beacon of hope for a renewed day. Climbing out of the valley of death was a possibility.

However, the challenges of mortality did not stop for Sally with the loss of one student.

A week later a dear friend died unexpectedly. As Sally dealt with her personal grief, yet another wave of death washed over the same high school. Three students were victims of a fatal car accident, and death had walked into the community and Sally's life again.

Bereavement affects everyone differently, but it does cast a shadow over even the most insensitive. As a trained professional, taught to deal with all kinds of challenges, Sally's heart had been brought to the breaking point. How would she climb out of the valley of death to see beyond hopelessness?

Sally understood running away from problems wouldn't be a solution because one takes problems along whether intentionally or not. However, Sally had a vacation planned immediately after the high school students died from the accident. She needed a break. As she drove from Michigan across Canada with a broken air conditioner in scorching heat, she found release and solace by singing herself into Vermont. Twelve hours of driving began a healing process with the added benefit of favorite tunes touching her soul and calming her heart. She would appreciate a visit to a country farm in New England.

Waking at dawn, the first morning at Patch Farm, the daylight showed Sally the sheep farm where she would be staying. The farm was nestled in a lush green valley. A wisp of fog blanketed the grazing sheep on the hillside outside her window. She listened to the melody of the busy birds. The song was a balm to soothe her soul from the tragedies of her preceding days and weeks. The inviting sights and sounds beckoned her out to a huge red barn where sheep were being milked to start the process of making cheese.

Once in the barn, she was assigned her morning tasks along with other guests—none of whom had farming experience. Sally was joined by two New York City educators who were as clueless as she was. They followed instructions and drove up the road to the "Maternity Ward" barn where they were to count the previous night's newly birthed lambs. As the sheep would say, with a bleat, it truly was the blind, leading the blind! The second location offered yet another picturesque setting: an open-ended barn against a steep hillside with sheep grazing beside their newborn lambs. Upon exiting the car, the sheep immediately began to baa, migrating toward the outbuilding.

First to reach the gate, Sally saw the lone ewe and her stillborn lamb lying next to her. The mother stood up as if to greet Sally and to show off her little one. Sally spoke her condolences to the grieving mother. Dealing with death for her had become so common, only this time she was talking to a ewe, yet it seemed oddly appropriate.

At the same time, Sally's human companions had jumped the fence and were up the hill for the counting. Sally kept vigil at the gate as the sheep from the hillside were flocking down into the barn vying to form a line—anxious to tell their version of the story better than their other wooly companions.

The sheep approached Sally from the opposite side of the barn from where the ewe kept vigil with her lamb. That side of the shelter was becoming very crowded. Eventually, the sheep funneled toward Sally single-file. One at a time, they took their turn and stood directly in front of her, looking her straight in the eyes and softly baaing. All the while, the mothers and siblings were loudly raising their voices in chorus in the background.

It seemed like all the sheep were anxious to tell Sally about this little lamb lying so still. As each one came up to her, she patted it on the head, assuring them one-by-one she saw and heard their cries and was sorry. Each would leave Sally, go to the stillborn, stop in front of it, pause in a bowing-like manner and then one by one quietly walk through the left side and out to the pasture. For Sally it was a stunning example of community grieving.

As the three unlikely farmer surrogates drove away, the grieving ewe stood guard waiting for the genuine farmer to come take care of her baby. As with human death, the family carried on beyond the community celebration and grieving.

Having been steeped in grief for weeks, Sally had come to a humble barn and found animals modeling: dying, death, grieving and getting on with life through grace, dignity and love. The sheep were compelled to tell their story, honor their dead loved one with great sincerity and respect, but then to get on with life. It was the inspiration she needed to leave the valley of death and climb the mountain of hope and life.

SOFT AWAKENING

Nancy Damon Burke

In the flash of time
between sleep and wake,
the haze is lifted
toward mindfulness.

Thoughts dance,
like ballerinas pirouetting
across a stage,
no clear destination.

Wisps of thought
form in pieces,
creating an elaborate
jigsaw puzzle.

Shifting, turning,
placing, replacing,
thoughts become ideas,
then plans.

A picture emerges.
Quietly forming, becoming vivid.
Full of promise
and potential.

Concentration creeps in
consciousness
tears
at the tranquil veil.

Dawn has broken.
That uniquely peaceful place,
gone 'til
another day is born.

MORE LOVE

Clare Green

Squished in the back seat of the Zdinak's station wagon, we were stopped at the pump of Frank's *Flying A* Garage, at the corner of Sharp Hill Road and Route 7 in Wilton, Connecticut. Frank, complete with a half-chewed stogie in his mouth with his perpetual dark, greased hands and face, bent his head toward the driver, Mr. Zdinak, and asked,

"Did you hear the news about David Hack Jr.?"

I noticed Mrs. Zdinak, seated in the passenger front seat, bending toward her husband while trying to wave her left arm to quiet Frank.

"Struck by lightning on Silvermine Golf Course. Dead."

I felt frozen in the moment while my mind raced to realize that, no wonder, I had a second sleep-over in a row this summer with my girlfriend, MaryAnne. My Mom had always enforced the family rule of one sleep-over per weekend.

I thought to myself, "My brother, dead?"
Frank wouldn't have noticed me in the back seat. The Zdinaks always had a carload of kids...seven to be exact.

It was summer, August 7, 1962. I was ten years old. Mrs. Zdinak turned to look at me in the back seat. I was barely breathing with clenched hands in my lap.

"The news is true. We're so sorry. Do you still want to go out to eat with us or go home now?

"Home please," I replied.

Thankful that Frank's Garage was just a half mile from my home, I thought, I can hold the tears until I'm home. May the gas tank fill-up quickly.

During the summer months, the neighborhood kids would ride our bikes to Frank's and spend a portion of our allowance on one-cent red cinnamon hotballs and pink Popeye Bubblegum wrapped with a cartoon. Frank kept his small assortment of candy in the glass display case near his cash register. We would wait until Frank could get out from working under a car to wait on us. Mom always told us not to interrupt his work and to be polite. He was the sole employee, owner, mechanic and gas attendant. Frank never showed if he was annoyed with us for coming down to spend five cents at a clip and interfering with his work days. He must have liked our small visits.

The gas tank was full. I was dropped home and comforted by my parents. News of my sixteen-year-old brother's death traveled fast by word of mouth and radio from Wilton, Connecticut. Our relatives in California heard about David's death on the news before we had the chance to reach them by phone. I found that fascinating. My brother made national news. Wow.

Over the ensuing few days the eventual sea of people that came to our house was like a rising high tide. During the wake, treasured memories, hugs from relatives, neighbors, and friends filled our hearts and warmed our home. Neighborly affections and kindnesses lingered for months afterwards. This late afternoon I felt unable to navigate easily in my own home.

"Wow, so crowded in here," I thought to myself, at age ten, as I tried to find Mom. The kitchen was filled with people and the countertops were piled high with an ample assortment of foods that amazed me, but no Mom. I wove my way through the dining room and through the ocean of friends and neighbors to finally find my mom seated and conversing in the living room.

As I approached, I heard her say, "David's death has brought more love into our family, not less."

My child-sized brain squirreled that phrase into my mind since it did not make sense to me.

"David was gone and there is more love, not less?" I thought to myself.

That felt contradictory to me, so I fashioned it to memory. I had been raised to believe in what my parents told me. Like a silent pearl of a seed, that one thought was planted in the garden of my heart. Unbeknownst to me, it germinated, flourished, and grew within me over the years. I would be reminded of those prophetic words time and again when loved ones passed from this earth and I was left here to grieve, appreciate, and still love. It would provide hope, acceptance, and understanding during the death of my beloved son years later.

"More love" did become evident as each family member became more grateful for the life of one another. No longer five siblings, but four. We grew in understanding of one another's differences. David's death reminded us that time on earth is precious and it is to be appreciated.

A month after David's death as I entered the fourth grade, I was still swept up in his dramatic exit from life. I remember storytelling it one day to my classmates while waiting in the bus line. Eager ears listened. I felt it was important to share his story. In a strange way, it made me feel special at a young age, since no one else could tell quite the same story:

"They were just getting off the golf course since the storm was brewing. One more green to putt, but that would be David's last. The lightning bolt hit him first, then traveled along the course, leaving a scorching scar on the ground, then up to the hip of his friend, Don Journey, where the bolt stopped. Don's leg was burned, but he survived. David's death was instantaneous. He lay there on the ground."

My own reflections of my brother's passing evolved with the passage of time. Brother David was my hero because he rescued me at a young age from a fluttering moth which was upsetting me. He cupped his hands, caught it and released it to the outdoors. Magic. Fear dissipated. My peace was restored. To this day, I still think of him when I catch and release a moth that has wandered into my home unannounced.

David had just given me my first driving lesson in the back fields on his restored old Model T chassis. I was so proud, even though shifting gears was difficult.

He was choreographer and performer in the local summer theatre's production of *The Boy Friend*. I felt lucky to have just seen it the weekend before.

Artistic and talented, David had renovated our home by painting and wallpapering rooms for Mom. David was Mom's right-hand handyman. He loved to help her in the home and he was talented at it. David also kept a sketch pad. Years later while perusing his sketches, I found a potentially prophetic colored chalk rendition of a man, wearing a light green toga from biblical times, walking down a long road with the bright sun ahead of him. I gave that drawing to brother Bill. David left us with a myriad of treasured memories and gifts. Simply, "more love" whispered to us.

As a child, I took solace in the company of silent prayers. Being clairvoyant since birth, I felt I lived in the company of ancestors, angels, and guardians. They were near to me if I needed them. I knew they were near by their whirling colors or by the soul songs I'd sing while waiting in the driveway for the bus. At a young age, I was beginning to learn that one of life's companions is constant change. Be open to change

During high school years my Uncle Oliver often wrote me letters. In one letter he tried to provide some comfort in regard to David's death. He stated, "A person's death does not end their life. Gifts and lessons from that person may still reach out to us. One needs only to be open to receive them. Life and death are intertwined. Entries and exits from this earth are perfectly timed."

Those words helped me to accept an eternal order to all of life. They gave my mind some hope and my heart some understanding.

Drops of wisdom watered my soul. Remain open to infinite connections.

Years later as a young mother, I wondered if there had been pain for David during his death. How was it for him? I was given insight during a meditation. There was no pain but rather a total oneness of illumination upon contact with the lightning and a bright, subsequent transition. He merged with the brilliance of light. This whisper of an insight gave me comfort and peace.

As my son, Ned David, grew and turned sixteen years old, I remembered thinking how my mom had to endure and let go of a vibrant life at this same age. No wonder she said that "David's death brings more love, not less."

Would my Mother have any idea that in thirty-nine subsequent years, I would have to endure a phone call to say that my son died on the table at the Conway Memorial Hospital in New Hampshire, from injuries sustained in an ice climbing accident? Her words reverberated through me as I tried to withstand the worst tsunami of my life. *Divine order, only love, more love,* became my gripping mantras so that I would not drown within this turbulent storm. I paced the kitchen floor and etched these phrases deep into my heart as I tried to make sense of Ned's dramatic exit from life.

Through the years I reflect upon the qualities of love, forgiveness, gratitude, and acceptance as key ingredients to healing an aching heart. Moments of denial, anger, and depression may occur but ultimately, one hopefully yields to the acceptance of tragedy. Acceptance leads to integrating the death experience into your life and transforming its difficult aspects into creative endeavors.

Sharing memories of the departed one with family and caring friends nourishes the strands of eternal connections, like a familiar piece of music that can be replayed and enjoyed. Peace and grace may prevail as by-products of a welcoming heart amidst the traumatic loss of a loved one.

Ned worshipped mountains. Immersed in nature's beauty his friends accompanied me to hike in the mountains to see the places where Ned worked and loved. These treks were a balm to my soul. Even the many humorous and adventure-filled stories about Ned breathed life into my heart. Signs, stories and conversations became reminiscent of "more love," in the wake of his passing.

I had kept the memory of Uncle David alive for my son, Ned David, in simple ways. Ned was born twelve years after David Jr.'s death. He was given his Uncle's name for his middle name: David, which means "Beloved."

I also told Ned how David loved old-fashioned cars and bought a Model T to restore it. I told him how he helped his Grandma Ginny with redecorating the family home that his Grandpa, nicknamed; *Chef Boy Our Dave*, built.

Amidst the parade of framed family photos on the wall, Ned saw David and me, as a young girl, at the Christmas table at Aunt Peg's and Uncle Robb's in Bronxville, New York. In that holiday moment David is bright-eyed and smiling, looking quite handsome in his tuxedo. I am looking down at my plate of food and wondering,"how am I ever going to eat this kidney pie? Do I have enough milk to drink to wash it down?" There's another black and white photo of David, and an even younger me, at four years old, sitting in the snow at the neighbors. There is a curious shaft of light in front of us. Another photo reminds us he was sitting in the driver's seat of his beloved restored car wearing his wool black and red lumberjack shirt with his cousin, Shelley Hack, as passenger. They both had wide smiles. It was a brilliant fall day. Through the years, these few photos wove us back to the beauty of David's love, his passions, and his short life on earth.

Now, David's photos are accompanied by numerous ones of my son Ned with family and friends. Cherished. When Ned's favorite season of winter approaches, I let the falling snow kiss my face as I turn heavenward or bury my face in the cold powder for its imprint, as he once taught me. Ned is smiling in my heart with all these moments and more. Gentle signs kindle the texture of infinite presence. Memory keeps the love in one's heart aglow.

I reflect, "Yes, Mother, there is more love, not less, with a loved one's passing." In death's wake, always invite "more love." The symphony of one's life does not end in death.

As Albert Einstein eternally reminds us, *make peace with your death, so that you might fully live.* May this story from my life gently catalyze your own reflections and meditations of the heart.

ECHOES OF MY SOUL

Sonya Shaw Wirtanen

Driving these roads
offers time to think.
Time to make sense of the footprints
left from the steps I have taken.

The Mountains of Mauna Loa standing tall,
strong and stable, lie to the East
The ocean in harmony with the moon,
the wind and the life that lives below, on the West.

The windows are down
sending my long blond hair across my eyes.
The scent of the sea is everywhere,
and the taste of salt still lingers on my lips.

Mountains, fields, ocean and road;
Heart, eyes, mind and spirit
all collide in the driver's seat.
The mirror reflects the roads that I crossed,

weaving East and West;
driving forward, but always looking behind.
The road ahead rounds over the setting sun,
bumping gently up and down.

The music sweetly plays
and rests softly in my mind.
His deep voice sings of Aina

and strums of dreams.

While the world around me displays
shades of green from earth and leaves,
hues of blue spread seamlessly from water to sky
filling my eyes with peace and wonder.

A clearing of palm trees peeks from the side of the road
inviting me to press the brakes.
Sweetly calling my name,
somehow knowing that I am searching for something.

I find myself traveling down
a long dirt road
towards the crashing waves.
Where a warm black rock quietly waits,

I take a well-worn pencil long forgotten
out of the glove box left there by another soul's journey.
To find the quiet space between our thoughts
we must allow those thoughts the attention they crave ---

Just for a moment.
I write.
The words are quick to enter my mind
quicker yet, to rest on the coffee stained scrap paper from beneath the
driver's seat.

Finding yourself is hard when
there are so many pieces missing.
Parts of me are nestled safely with my mother,
while others have been sent to soar with my father.

Pieces of me lie with my sisters,
my friends,
the man with whom I have built my life.
Then there is the piece of me,

desperately tethered tightly to *him*.
These pieces wait patiently
as I am scattered across this Earth
stretching over 5000 square miles.

To find yourself when lost,
is to seek the point
where the ocean meets the sky;
Or the place where mountains gather at the earth.

The sun sets gently in front of me
disappearing behind the cliffs.
Feeling lost and found,
waiting, while time stands still for me.

Nowhere to go,
yet nowhere to stay.
I am somewhere between
the salt and the sand.

Along the roots of these trees,
atop the waves of the sea,
traveling up the mountain to look below
through the eyes of the stars,

into the unknown places where our spirit resides.
It is there I shall rest.
For that is why I am here,
listening to the echoes of my soul.

BEYOND THE FARAWAY ROOM

Mary Louise Owen

Ordinarily timid, five-year-old Louise Willow was downright frightened and nervous. She was a total coward, even for a little girl, as the bedtime hour approached. Here she was again, facing sleep time alone in *that* room at her grandparents' house.

Louise's native Scottish grandparents lived on an island blanketed with a quiet country setting. It was the house her mother was born in. This place was so different from Louise's suburban ranch-style home across the waters of Puget Sound in Seattle. Louise dreaded the climb up the dark narrow stairway to the second floor, always hoping there would be no surprises along the way. Plagued with imaginings, she was terrified of the unknown—sure to die from whatever may jump out at her in that dimly lit hall on the way to the dreaded bedroom.

The assigned sleeping area was determined by Louise's history of bedwetting. It was far from a secret in the family and most certainly a mantle of shame to Louise. The disgrace especially stung when her grandmother would proclaim in her thick Scottish brogue, in front of whomever was visiting at bedtime, "Louise, you sleep in the Faraway Room, so you won't spoil a good bed." Her grandmother seemed to feel the need to announce this each visit.

The humiliation was one thing, but the fear of the bedroom was altogether another. Louise felt so alone as she slowly ascended the steep dark stairway, creeping with caution toward the dreaded chamber. The adults' expectation was that she could and should conquer any fears that may haunt her imagination and put herself to bed without assistance.

However, just the name, 'Faraway Room' seemed to conjure images of goblins and ghosts with each calculated step. Not only was creeping down that hallway scary, but to make matters worse, eyeing Louise from inside the Faraway room was Chief Seattle, dressed in all his finest warrior regalia! Chief Seattle's looming portrait terrified Louise! What if there were Indians waiting for her arrival? Why, they may take her away, maybe even have her for dinner. After all Chief Seattle and his Indians were wild, weren't they?

Once in the room, after checking under the bed, behind the dresser and out the window, Louise settled in and tried to fall asleep. Although her fears were somewhat allayed, sleep evaded her until, to her surprise, she found herself waking to a new day and a chance to scurry out of the Faraway Room and Chief Seattle's daunting gaze.

The Faraway Room seemed a punishment, a banishment from the family. For Louise, adopted into the family as an infant, this was interpreted by her childish emotions as not measuring up to family standards. As Louise matured, the Faraway Room became a challenge to her sense of risk-taking in life. Where could she go beyond the Faraway Room? Who and what other than darkness or an Indian chief figure would Louise encounter? How would she be able to survive?

In hindsight, Louise realized that at age five, while enduring the fears of banishment, she could never have dreamed of the wonderful adventures that would lie beyond that imposing Faraway Room. As time went by, she came to realize, the Faraway Room not only harbored the fears of a child, but planted the seeds to develop strength, courage, and tenacity to live beyond the terrors and loneliness of childhood imagination. Eventually, Louise stepped onto the path of an unimaginable lifetime journey—beyond the feared Faraway Room.

TENTATIVE BRAVERY

Linda J. Donaldson

Taking first steps—breaking sobbing breaths
Wondering out loud, fear of being proud
Gathering frayed thread unraveling in my head
Courage twinkles faintly, enabling a mighty stretch

To be, to want to be, independently me
A dangerous question: what do I need?
A mind free of insults, thoughts without shackles
Struggles ensue, unsure what to do

Dangerous entanglements to shed and get through
Now on the other side, tingling with incipient pride
Wanting easy happiness, sensing that it's near
Craving a life lived without fear

Having achieved what I'd believed unattainable
Tending my garden and breathing in easy strides
If you're afraid, if you're trampled too
Remember I did it and so can you

VISUAL LINES

Steven Michaels

I believed
I could *ALtER rEaliTy*.

It happened
for the *briefest*
of moments.

Unfocusing
my e y e s
to stare
at the *Vertices*
of **my bedroom,**
a **Blinding Light**
s p r e a d f o r t h
from the *cracks*
in the Fabric of
　　　　Reality.

For this **Light**
felt like the one
people claim to see
before D y i n g.
So I stopped **in alarm**
too afraid,
believing
it would beckon me **Home**
Or to some ***ethereal*** *Dimension*.

Trying it
a second time
I　　　　　　laughed
for **Logic** had taken over
and the **Power--**
I knew
was g o n　e.

THE CONFIDANTE

Maggie Scarf

Our house had a coal furnace and every evening my mother went down to the cellar to fill it up. I often came down to listen to stories of her life with rapturous adoration. To me they were like the magical tales of Schereherazade. As she spoke, the flames from the furnace played across her beautiful aquiline features. I was breathless with love and hope – hope that some distant future happiness would await her.

My mother was my father's third wife. She was a full generation younger. His first wife had divorced him. His second wife was my mother's older sister. She had had four children who were close to my mother's age, but I never met them. They broke off all relations with my harsh, miserly father as soon as they were self-supporting.

My mother hadn't wanted to marry my father. When he came to Europe to claim her as the sister of his dead wife – in accordance with the Jewish tradition of maintaining the bloodline – she protested that she was too young to be mated with this gruff, domineering elderly man. But my grandmother was a widow, and the dry goods store she owned was barely earning enough for the family food. The decision was out of her hands. My mother had to go.

On the eve of her departure, a gypsy had told my mother's fortune. She predicted an unhappy marriage and four children. In the flickering lights from the coal heater, my mother spoke with great excitement about how many of the gypsy's prophecies had come to pass. She did have an unhappy marriage. She did have four children. She told me the gypsy also predicted that she would marry a second time. This time she would be idyllically happy.

How joyful that made me feel! "One day you will be happy, Mommy," I told her, enthralled by the belief that this second marriage would come to pass.

She would take me on her lap and tell me other stories. My favorite was about how much the captain of the boat who had brought her to America had admired her. The special attentions he had paid to her. Well, she was very beautiful. I wondered why that captain hadn't saved her. Why hadn't he whisked her off before she disembarked and fell into her doomed wifehood?

One morning I came across a contest on a cereal box that asked contestants to finish a random monthly statement "in 25 words or less." The entrant that came up with the perfect statement could win a real diamond ring. I could give it to my mother. Each time a new cereal box appeared on the kitchen table, I entered the contest. I must have entered it dozens of times, but the perfect sentence eluded me.

Perhaps the most rapturous experience of my childhood was one New Year's Eve. My mother took my little brother and me down to the center of Philadelphia for the New Year's Eve celebration. Melvin must have been about five, which made me eight years old, or so. We traveled on the number fifty-four trolley car. When we alighted from the trolley, our small selves mingled with the legs of the milling crowds. As midnight struck that evening, we looked heavenward to see the flowering designs of the fireworks. I was thunderstruck. Each outburst was more intricate and beautiful than the preceding one. I remember little else from that evening except my eyes slowly closing as we rode home on the trolley. I slumped against my mother as I fell into her arms.

FLOWERS FOR THE DEVIL

Dennis F. King

Looking down from my guard tower one day

at Spandau Prison in Berlin, Germany.

 Only one inmate remaining there.

Tending to his manicured flower bed.

He got down on his knees, as if praying,

to weed this little plot.

This scene, rooted in my mind,

for over forty years.

The irony of this devil named Rudolf Hess,

a Nazi leader, stopping to smell the roses.

Serving out his solitary life sentence

until the day he hung himself.

Forty years.

Not one tear shed.

Flower bed plowed under,

 the very next day.

THE WHITCOMB INN

Nancy Damon Burke

As she straightened her desk, Wendy Buchanan was thinking of the long trip to Maine in front of her. The latest weather forecast was predicting a storm and she wanted to beat it if she could. Grabbing her coat, she poked her head into her boss's office.

"I'm heading out, Mrs. Green."

"Have a safe trip, Wendy. Make sure you stop for the night if the weather gets too bad."

"Oh, don't worry, I will," said Wendy, knowing that Mrs. Green would worry, nevertheless.

The Green Insurance Company's office was a home away from home. The staff was a close-knit group and felt almost like family. They were happy that Wendy had finally decided to take her vacation leave and go away for three weeks. She had never done that before. She rarely took even one week, so taking three weeks was unheard of. The whole office was excited for Wendy and told her so.

Her car was packed, and she was soon on the way out of town. Wendy liked to drive the backroads and not the interstate highways. In the summer, she stopped at old variety stores and antiques shops along the way. She rarely made the trip in the winter and decided she'd better take the easiest route with the current forecast. Wendy traveled down Route 2 heading to Route 495. As she entered the interstate, snowflakes danced around lightly, but they didn't stick to the windshield. She was glad that it wasn't dark yet and the driving was easy.

Singing along with the radio, Wendy almost missed the ring of her cellphone. It was her friend Cindy checking on her progress. Cindy's family had an inn on the ocean and were expecting her early that evening. She assured her that she was on target and would be there right on schedule. She heard Cindy's dad holler in the background that they had a fire in the fireplace and marshmallows for her hot chocolate. She couldn't wait.

Wendy had been going to the Whitcomb Inn as long as she could remember. Her parents had taken the family there for two weeks every year in July. She grew up getting to know the coast of Maine. Cindy had a room to herself but was a little jealous of her brothers because they slept in the bunk room with their friends. They all did odd jobs around the inn to earn spending money. They rode their bikes into town to spend it at the Harbour Bay General Store. The penny candy, comic books, and movie rentals kept them entertained in the evenings until they were teenagers. This was typical of most kids in town. They were free to roam within reason. Their parents had done the same thing in their day and wanted them to live the carefree summer life that they had. Every parent knew that life got harder too soon.

When her brother John turned sixteen, he got his license, and a car. John took them to the drive-in theater every Friday night. They packed as many kids into the car as they possible could. A couple of times, they hid extras in the trunk. Their parents heard what they were doing and put an end to it. Nobody wanted to be in there anyway, so they only did it twice.

Eventually, John started hanging out with an older crowd and spent more time with them. He had a new girlfriend named Candy who Wendy and Cindy didn't like at all. She hung on John's arm, gazed up at him, and called him Johnny. She told the girls to stop asking him for rides. She wanted to go to the drive-in with him alone and didn't want them around. They didn't tell John what she said but didn't ask him for rides anymore.

Cindy was disappointed in her brother when he came home with hickies on his neck. Her friend Audrey told her that there was a name for girls that gave hickies, but she wouldn't tell what it was. Wendy and Cindy really wanted to know, so they decided to ask one of the older girls who worked part-time at the library. She read lots of books and might know about hickies. They would ask her when no one else was around and they learned a lot.

The last summer they were all together, John took them to the beach. They threw a Frisbee, built elaborate sand castles, and in the evening, had a gigantic bonfire. Some of John's friends brought beer and a bottle of rum. Wendy took a sip of the rum and didn't like it. She took a beer to wash it down and didn't like that either. She and Cindy sipped a little more just to fit in but couldn't stand the taste. The guys seemed to like it a lot. Before long they were stumbling drunk. All the kids had a curfew of ten o'clock and it was getting close. John said he would drive them home. Cindy tried to tell him that he couldn't drive after drinking, but he said he was fine. Wendy said she would walk home, and Cindy agreed. It was a long walk, but they didn't want to ride with John.

The accident had been a fiery wreck. John had swerved into the passing lane. The tractor trailer could not avoid hitting them. John and Candy were killed instantly. Jimmy and Greg were life-flighted to Portland and died after being in comas for weeks. Cindy's brothers Alan and David lived but still have handicaps due to their injuries. That crash changed the lives of both families forever.

Wendy shook her head and cleared the images of that time out of her mind. She looked forward to seeing the inn with all its changes. The Whitcomb brothers ran it now. They had made many improvements over the years. Each brother had spent long painful hours in rehab after the accident. They had worked hard to become the carpenters that they are today. Despite losing part of an arm in the crash Alan could still wield a hammer with the best of them. And David's leg would never be perfect, but his limp didn't prevent him from climbing ladders.

They started with buying one house at a time and renovating it for sale. They made more money with each one and after a few years hired local teenagers and showed them the ropes. Their only requirements were that they would be clean and sober and willing to learn. They had no problem finding new hires. They had a list of hopefuls from families who wanted their kids to work with the Whitcomb's. It was just as normal to see a teenage girl with a carpenter's belt on her hips, as it was a boy.

Wendy was entering the Maine Turnpike just as the snow started coming down harder. The wind had picked up and it was difficult to see the road. She was glad that there were other cars so she could follow their tail lights. It made her chuckle a bit to think that she might follow them right off the road if they went into a slide. She was glad she had purchased new snow tires a week ago.

Slowing down, Wendy realized that she was getting close to her exit. If she missed it, there would not be another for miles. She stayed in the right lane and eased into the turn when she reached the exit. She was shocked to see a dark figure standing in the road. He had his thumb out and Wendy assumed he must be a hitchhiker. Knowing she would spin out if she slammed on the brakes, she pumped them and tried to avoid hitting the man. She didn't hit him but slid off into the snowbank. As she tried to back out, her tires started to spin and she couldn't move at all.

Just then the dark figure appeared at her window. He told her to try rocking back and forth and he would push her out. A little afraid, she decided she had no alternative. She couldn't get the car out by herself. She did what he said and soon she was back on the road. Biting her tongue and swallowing hard, she asked him if he needed a ride. He seemed puzzled that she would offer and said that he did. Brushing the snow off his coat and stamping his feet, he slid into the passenger seat.

Wendy asked the stranger where he was going and he replied, "to the Whitcomb Inn." She told him he was in luck; she was headed there too. He went on to tell her that he had been saved by the Whitcomb brothers. He'd been an alcoholic for nearly twenty years and had finally gone to rehab in Maine. He said that his name was William but he went by Liam, adding that he'd shortened it when he got sober.

He had spent a year at the inn and now he was doing what he loved. In the summer months he painted landscapes on Cape Cod in Massachusetts. In the winter, he painted crashing waves and the rocky coast of Maine. He sold paintings of lighthouses to tourists to make a living. For one month, each winter, he went to the Whitcomb Inn and taught painting classes. It was his way of saying thank you for his sobriety. He saw how Alan and David had turned their lives around and he was grateful. Wendy was glad she had broken her "never pick up a hitchhiker" rule and had given him a lift.

Pulling into the parking lot of the inn, the sight took Wendy's breath away. This was not the Whitcomb Inn of her memory. It was huge, and more than that, it was beautiful. There was a wide porch around the front of the house. Rocking chairs and benches with pillows were grouped for conversation. Paths, framing a massive garden that had been put to bed for the winter, covered acres of land. Each plot had been carefully blanketed with straw, waiting for spring. The inn and surrounding land had been transformed. There were cottages dotting the landscape and people rushing in and out of the cold. Couples seemed to be heading toward the main house.

Wendy started unloading the car and Liam grabbed the suitcases. He dropped them in the vestibule and ran back for more. He wondered how long Wendy was planning to stay. She had several heavy suitcases and he thought she might be there for the winter. He had his belongings shipped by UPS when he traveled. His paint box was his most valued possession, and he couldn't chance it being damaged on the road. It was easy and practical to ship and was always waiting for him on arrival, wherever he went.

An elderly artist he'd met in his travels had given him the box because his hands were crippled with arthritis and he could no longer paint. It was a treasure. The old man told of his fascinating adventures and how he'd painted birds all over the world. The story long told in his family was that he was a distant cousin of Monet. His name was Claude also. Liam believed it and tried to put at least one bird in all his paintings in tribute to his friend. He had been captivated by the

Impressionist style ever since his grandfather bought him a print of Monet's Japanese gardens.

Cindy's dad opened the door with a flourish and welcomed them both in. He told them to put their bags by the stairs and come sit by the fire. Hot chocolate was waiting on the warmer and the cookies smelled like Christmas. Wendy put her feet up and relaxed for the first time in weeks. She had to concentrate to keep from nodding off.

A young couple came down the stairs and quietly asked her if she knew where the AA meeting was. David had closed the doors to an adjoining room and Wendy guessed that it might be in there. She opened the door to inquire. There were several couples sitting together on couches and singles sitting on comfortable chairs around the room. David motioned for the young couple to come in. Cindy sat in a chair by the door and was surprised as Alan Whitcomb stood up by the fireplace and started speaking.

"Hi, I'm Alan, and I'm an alcoholic."

He went on to say that he'd been sober for almost nineteen years and was still taking it one day at a time. He was looking forward to a twenty year coin in the coming year. Other members of the group spoke about their addiction and how the Whitcomb Inn had been the place they'd come to kick the habit. Many had come back after several failed attempts at sobriety. They all agreed that they were one drink away from failing again. At this moment, most were sober.

Liam stood up and spoke with a strong clear voice. He seemed like a shy man in most surroundings, but he was proud of this accomplishment and happy to share the experience of sobriety. He told his story of being at rock bottom and the difficulty of rising up. What had seemed like a mountain those years ago, was still a mountain today, but easier now to climb.

Holding her breath, Wendy ran up to her room and opened her suitcase. She dug under the jeans and sweaters and pulled out the bottles of vodka that she'd so carefully packed. She cracked the seal on the first bottle and lifted it to her lips. She wanted to take a pull on that bottle as a baby to the breast. She needed it, and she needed it now.

Something stopped her. To this day, she can't say exactly what it was. She had hidden her addiction so well, her co-workers didn't know, her family never suspected and Cindy surely never did--or did they? She took both bottles into the bathroom and poured them down the sink.

Running down the stairs, she tripped and fell. Ironically, the only way was up. Wendy quietly opened the door to the meeting and sat in the back row. Liam was standing in the front and had just finished speaking. He nodded toward Wendy and smiled. She took a deep breath, squared her shoulders and walked to the front of the room.

"Hi, I'm Wendy, and I'm an alcoholic."

A SIMPLE PRAYER

Karyl J. Leslie

(see Matthew 12:18-21, Isaiah 42:1-4)

I pray for the bruised reed
and the dimly burning wick,
including those who don't realize their brokenness.

I pray for God's reviving
and the healing that is needed,
including for those who don't realize it or admit it
even to themselves:

those whose bravado is overwhelming,
those who inflict hurt and brokenness
in their own hurt and brokenness.

I pray for all the bruised reeds
and the dimly burning wicks.

I pray for God's reviving of the core of love,
and for the healing,
and enlightening
that is needed.

MORNING GLORY INCIDENT

Linda Donaldson

In 1982, I lived in Virginia in a house that my ex-husband bought—which I never saw until he'd arranged the mortgage. I secretly bought a package of morning glory seeds and planted them below the kitchen window. I'd also planted tulips under the kitchen window, between the house and the driveway.

Daniel didn't want flowers. He thought only vegetables were worth the work of gardening.

When those tulips bloomed that spring, I was thrilled. He just mumbled. When he was ready to plant his vegetable garden, he had a load of railroad ties delivered to make a raised bed. He had the deliverymen offload those stinky, sticky ties right on top of my beautiful tulips. They had only just started to bloom! I felt as crushed as they looked. But I knew the morning glories would still grow, and I fixed string from the kitchen window down to the stakes in the dirt so they'd have a place to twine.

They came up, all blue and pink and gorgeous. I watched as they twisted their way up the string toward my kitchen window. I loved seeing them bouncing there in the breeze. While washing the dishes, I could look out and see the lovely blooms. Then he started in.

"Those morning glory vines are going to grow into the bricks and ruin the mortar," he growled through gritted teeth.

I was still a little brave back then. "Oh, don't be ridiculous." I snapped back. "They're growing on the string, for goodness' sake."

I didn't realize, though I should have, that he knew those flowers were one of the only things that gave me pleasure. He'd systematically arranged our world so that only he could be the focus of my thoughts and feelings. Phone calls with my sisters were cut short. He'd continuously belittled my job. Any friendships that I tried to make were quickly destroyed when he'd made lecherous comments.

He was jealous of those morning glories and wasn't going to rest until he'd defeated them. His anger about them escalated and was unrelenting. I'd welcome him home from work and he'd immediately start begrudging the morning glories.

"They're an eyesore," he'd insisted. "Ruining the whole side of the house."

"Oh, Daniel, I don't want to argue with you," I'd pleaded. "There are only three tiny strings, just don't look at them."

"I have to park over there." He'd say through clenched teeth. "It's the first thing I see when I come home. I can't just ignore those hideous things."

He scowled and grumbled, not even saying anything good about the special effort I'd put into making dinner just the way he liked it. Carrots had to be sliced so that each piece was identical to all the others; not too thick but not too thin. Steak had to be just the right cut and cooked perfectly to medium rare. Serving bowls had to be warmed and the table had to be set precisely to his exacting standards. Not a word of praise would pass his lips as we ate in sullen silence.

He was Jesuit-trained in the art of logic. You could not win an argument with him. He would go for the jugular no matter how inane the subject. I once witnessed him cajole his five-year-old nephew into ceding a point through bribery. He was relentless and ruthless.

The morning glory debate became an everyday argument, and I wasn't strong enough to keep sticking up for myself. Eventually, he wore me down.

One Saturday in August, as the blooms were full among the shiny heart-shaped leaves, he stomped into the house shouting, "You waste so much time on those flowers when you should be pruning my tomatoes and watering the pepper plants." He shook a trowel an inch from my face, and I could see the muscles clenching his jaws.

I still regret stomping out to the side yard and ripping those morning glories up by their roots when they were in the prime of their blooming. I cried miserably, but I did it. He drove me to it. But *I* did it. There are few things I regret more in life than destroying those poor morning glories in a vain effort to save my doomed marriage.

• • •

Years later, while speaking with my counselor at the Women's Resource Center, I described this to the counselor's amazement. She asked me why I didn't just let him be angry with me. Now, looking back, this seems like a reasonable question. Nobody can imagine how dangerous it was for Daniel to get angry. It was life threatening. He'd even endangered his own mother with a carving knife once when she'd crossed his will. With normal people, you endure their anger, they get over it and life goes on. With Daniel, you did everything and anything to avoid a wrath that could shatter your ego and your well-being. To appease him, I pulled my morning glories up and, of course, it still wasn't enough to make him happy.

I bought my very own house long after the divorce. Today, my front garden patch is bursting with snapdragon blooms, dahlias, gladiola, four o'clocks, dianthus, thunbergia, cosmos, impatiens and zinnia. Of course, I have three kinds of morning glories climbing over the roof of my screen porch. All summer, humming birds sip nectar from their blossoms.

FIRST LOVE

Mary Louise Owen

Bad boys can be tantalizing and, oh, so intriguing. Their charm and captivating personality can send a call into the universe—entrapping the good Christian girl. Unaware, she can easily be enticed to abandon some of the upstanding moral fibers her parents weaved within her for years. Ray Akers was that bad boy who snagged Katie Beth's attention. At least, in her parents' minds, he was a bad boy, but Katie Beth begged to differ.

The infatuation was born at first sight in a tiny high school, long since closed. The small town of Twisp was nestled in the foothills of the Cascade Mountain Range among apple orchards in eastern Washington State. The year was 1966. Katie Beth was a sophomore and Ray was a senior. Katie Beth's dad had acquired a new position in the local bank. Moving from a large Seattle high school, Katie Beth experienced a huge shift in her education experience, but most notably, her social life. Although the school was extremely small, with class sizes between twenty and thirty students, there was one who stood out to Katie Beth. Ray's imposing six feet, five-inch height was only surpassed by his welcoming, wide grin. With his head cocked to the side, and his mischievous eyes sparkling, Ray's deep voice smoothly said, "Well, hello there."

Summer joy for most of the teens in Twisp consisted of cruising the town streets, swimming in the river, hanging out at the drive-in, and going to dances at the Grange Hall. Oh, and occasionally there would be night-time parking at the ski slope. Katie Beth gained popularity as she drove her '38 lackluster yellow De Soto, which accommodated a gaggle of teens in the humongous back seat. The town was small, but the fun was plentiful.

Joy for Katie Beth was time spent with Ray. He worked in the summer as a firefighter for the National Forest Service. He was often taken by air and parachuted to certain locations to fight fires. Katie Beth didn't see him too often in the summertime. When he was in town, they went to the dance, for part of the evening anyway.

One day, they had gone riding on Ray's motorcycle. This was one of the acts that categorized Ray as a "bad boy" in the eyes of Katie Beth's parents. She had been forbidden to ride motorcycles.

She thought, *what they don't know won't hurt them.*

With fleeting hesitation, she went ahead—enjoying the ride out in the forest with her heartthrob until they had a slight spill on a rough patch of trail. Neither of them broke anything, but Katie Beth got a huge burn on her calf that summer shorts did not hide. To make matters worse, she stayed out past curfew on a night when her parents had out-of-town overnight guests. To her parents, the humiliation of a daughter out of control was unthinkable.

Still, Katie Beth and Ray dated for several years, even after he graduated and went on to Idaho State College. Two years later she enrolled in Washington State University which was located seven miles from Ray. Of course, Katie Beth's parents weren't too happy about that. However, pride trumped concern since Katie Beth was the first in her family to go to college.

One snowy weekend, Ray talked Katie Beth into going home to Twisp to watch his brother play in a basketball tournament. By this time, Katie Beth's family had moved back to Seattle, so they would not be there. Katie Beth made the decision that there was no need to inform them of this hundred-mile, forty-eight-hour weekend jaunt that she and Ray were taking.

After all, Katie Beth thought, *I'm over eighteen and I have a place to stay. What could happen, anyway?*

The basketball games were filled with excitement and the Twisp team won the State "B" Class Championship. Celebration was on. Leaving the town where the deciding game was played, the celebrants headed back to Twisp. Katie Beth, Ray, and two other couples stuffed into a pea green two-door Pontiac. Katie Beth sat on Ray's lap in the back seat behind the driver. Another couple filled the passenger side of the back while Ray's brother Bruce and his girlfriend were in the front. Also, a half keg of beer rested on the passenger side floor which would be opened later.

It was a joyous ride. Bruce took a turn off the main highway and headed onto a mountain road which was considered the back way to Twisp. It was a beautifully cold, clear night with snow piled high along both sides of the road. The view, even in the dark, was magnificent. Stars shone brightly with a hint of the aurora borealis dancing in the deep blue sky. Suddenly, the car swerved—breaking the barrier of snow with the front left tire. The car stopped, resting only on snow banks. Katie Beth looked out the window from the back seat and could see below, *way* below. They had a problem, there were only two doors and one was over a cliff. How were they going to get out of this mess?

Quiet terror enveloped the crowded car. How were they to escape without tipping the front end of the car over the precipice? After all, the snow bank, along with the weight of four people in the back seat, was the only thing keeping the vehicle from tumbling down the steep rock face. Without speaking, they all knew this could result in devastation, even death.

Bitterly cold, the car holding the youthful troupe captive was located miles from any town or even a single house. To make matters worse, the clothing and shoes worn were inadequate for the situation. The girls were outfitted in knee length dresses and high heeled shoes, common for that era on a date night.

Automatically, Katie Beth turned her thoughts to prayer – her usual first step in difficult times. Comforting words from the 91st Psalm flooded her mind. *He that dwelleth in the secret place of the Most High shall abide under the shadow of the Almighty. I will say of the Lord, He is my refuge and my fortress; my God in Him I trust."*

She added, *Surely, he will deliver me from this mess!*

In contrast to Katie Beth's faith solution, two of the three engineering students put their practical knowledge to the test. With care, a strategy was put into place. Executing the plan was the tricky part.

Bruce and Janice, the couple in the front seat, carefully exited through the only door hovering over solid ground, landing with their feet firmly planted. The car rocked slightly. The sound of cold snow crunched with the contact of their bodies and the shift of weight against the metal of the vehicle. Their footsteps sounded disconcerting to those left in the teetering car. Once out, the couple retreated to the back of the vehicle. They carefully perched themselves on the trunk with the hope of displacing the weight of those about to spill out of the back seat. As the shifting settled, with caution, the back seat was pushed forward, first allowing the girls trapped in the back to come forward. They exited one at a time, prudently stepping up and through the doorway to safety. Each in turn weighted the back of the car down with their bodies on the trunk from the outside.

Once the last two guys, Ray and Arnie, were out, the car needed to be moved so that all four wheels were on solid ground. For that to happen, since the troupe could not get in front to push it back on the road, they had to pull the car. By opening the trunk, three people grasped the inside lip and pulled as hard as they could—backing up one step at a time. In the same moment, one of the guys used his body weight to push from the opened passenger doorway toward the road.

Looking back, Katie Beth liked to think that her prayerful petition for God to hold them under his wings of protection helped make the difference. She also knew that her friends' careful, thoughtful planning and swift and cautious actions saved them from what could have been a tragic outcome.

The next day following their cliff-hanging adventure, Ray and Katie Beth headed back to their perspective colleges and studies. The return trip was unremarkable. Kathie Beth's parents were kept in the dark, forever. It wasn't an adventure Katie Beth was willing to divulge.

In the months that followed, the couple spent many weekends together. As time went on, it was becoming clear to Katie Beth that Ray was beginning to use drugs. That was a line Katie Beth did not want to cross. She had seen first-hand what happened to a family friend who had taken a bad trip down the drug road. At first she confronted him, then flushed his stash down the toilet. Of course, that didn't go too well. From then on, their relationship began to deteriorate. Soon, their times together became less frequent and Ray eventually admitted that he was seeing a mutual friend of theirs.

Not only was Katie Beth's relationship with Ray fading, she realized too, that she was going to have to drop out of college for lack of funds. Her parents were not able to co-sign a student loan at the time and Katie Beth could not find a part-time job that would bring in adequate funds to cover her costs. It was time to put college on hold and cut the cord with Ray. Moving home to her parents and securing a local job seemed the appropriate strategy.

The night before leaving college, Katie Beth and Ray had a heart to heart conversation.

To Katie Beth's surprise, Ray said, "You are lucky that you believe in God. I just can't see it. But I see how it helps you in your life. Hang onto to that Katie Beth. Don't let it go. Your faith is important to you." She had no idea how much those words would revisit her for years to come.

The day came when Katie Beth was to return home from college, Ray had arranged for her to accompany him up in a skydiving plane prior to her taking off in a passenger plane for Seattle. With fear-filled anticipation, she donned the outfit—including the parachute required of any person along for the ride. Climbing into the plane, she was surprised that there were no seats—just an empty belly of a space.

Carefully, Ray instructed Katie Beth on what to do when he jumped out of the airplane.

He said, "As soon as I jump, you need to lean out over the doorway of the plane, so you have a clear view to see me falling and watch my parachute open."

Katie Beth was afraid of heights, she was terrified to even climb up bleachers at the basketball games. *How was she going to lean out of a plane in the sky?* she thought.

To her shock, Katie Beth found herself following Ray's directions. After all, what was the point of going up to say, "goodbye" if she didn't follow through? Ray's intention was for the farewell to be a dramatic ending to their four-year relationship. She was also astonished by the rush of adrenaline she felt as she carefully crawled to the opening and gazed into the vast sky. Not only was Ray's decent breathtaking, but the general atmosphere in the sky was welcoming, almost enticing her to jump. Understanding Ray's love for skydiving dawned on Katie Beth as her fears fled. She basked in the moment of spacious sky splendor, and a final farewell to her first love.

August 13, 2000 from Gray Knob Shelter Journal where Ned Green spent the weekend as Caretaker in Northern Presidential Mountains of NH:

"My stay, however brief, has come to a close, and the cabin is silent except for a drip into an empty bucket. Clouds outside swallow up the mountains and freeze them in their belly. One week left in these gorgeous mountains.

The summer is gone, fall creeps in clutching the ragged tendril of a beaten gortex parka. Apple cider, maple leaves and the promise of a cold winter.

Ah, New England and a tinge of romanticism races through my bones."

Enjoy People,
Ned

OUR CONTRIBUTORS

THE FOUNDER OF QUABBIN QUILLS

Steven Michaels is the author of *Sweet Life of Mystery*, a parody of the whodunit genre. He has been featured on *The Satirist* website for his scintillating take on current affairs and has written over twenty plays for students as school director for the Drama Club. Steve founded the Quabbin Quills to ensure that the art of writing would long endure in and around this area for many years to come. He and other writers featured in this book came together to showcase the talent of local authors in their second anthology, Mountains and Meditations.

ABOUT OUR PUBLISHER

Garrett Zecker is the publisher and co-founder of Quabbin Quills. He holds an MA in English from Fitchburg State University and an MFA in Fiction from Southern New Hampshire University's Mountainview MFA. He founded Perpetual Imagination in 2004, specializing in independent releases and live events. Garrett is a writer, actor, and teacher of writing and literature. Links to much of his work, including other publications, full Shakespeare In The Park performances, and hundreds of book and movie reviews can be found at his blog, **GarrettZecker.com**.

ABOUT OUR ILLUSTRATOR

North Quabbin resident **Emily Boughton** has been rooted in the worlds of art and literature throughout her life. Her most prominent project to date is the interactive book and exhibit *Figure Me Out*, where she merges her love of design, photography, and writing into a self-reflective experience. When she is not working with youth at her local library, Emily enjoys filling her latest sketchbook with new ideas and doodles.

ABOUT OUR EDITORS

Linda Donaldson is a graduate of the University of Massachusetts and former editor of the RVDA News. She is an educator and has been recognized by Literacy Volunteers of America for her devotion to tutor training. Linda is a proud homeowner in Athol where she works as an executive secretary. She is an avid reader who enjoys gardening, family gatherings, and mystery rides.

Clare Green of Warwick is an author and educator, and has been clairvoyant since childhood. She offers her insights silently or verbally when asked. Clare welcomes folks to enjoy a cup of tea while visiting her fairy cottage or walk the woodland labyrinth for peace and reflection.

Diane Kane is submissions coordinator and treasurer for Quabbin Quills. She helped to produce both *Time's Reservoir Anthology* as well as *Mountains and Meditations.* Diane also writes food review articles for the Uniquely Quabbin Magazine. Her latest accomplishment is a self-published book of flash fiction stories, *Flash in the Can,* available on Amazon.com. You can follow Diane on Facebook at "PageofPossibilities" or online at **WriteofPossiblities.com**

James Thibeault is the author of the novel *Deacon's Folly,* as well as the author of several short stories that have appeared in many literary journals and anthologies. He has been an English teacher for just under a decade and has been a resident of Massachusetts for all of his life.

Charlotte Taylor has published both short stories and poetry. She loves the process of creating with words and enjoys sharing the craft of writing with others. Charlotte is the writing persona for *OPENArt+Yoga* and is an active blogger for her work in Ayurveda, yoga, and writing. She is actively seeking a life of peace, study, and fun. Charlotte can often be found surrounded by cats with a mug of tea and reading books. Other times, you'll find her climbing mountains or crawling under barbed wire. Read more at **MusingClio.wordpress.com**.

Michael Young began writing in college in Spokane, Washington. While in graduate school at Princeton, he was invited to submit poems to the student publication, *The Wineskin*. Recently, he has been published in *A Time for Singing* and *A Certain Slant*. In 2013 he won first place in the Millers River Watershed Council's River Verses Contest with "The Lure," which is republished in this book.

ABOUT OUR AUTHORS

Jon Bishop is a Massachusetts-based writer and poet. He is co-editor and co-founder of *Portrait of New England* and co-founder of *The JT Lit Review*, a literary blog. His work has appeared in *The Arts Fuse, Fourth & Sycamore, Laurel Magazine, Boston Literary Magazine, Liberty Island*, and *Burning House Press*, among other publications. His first book of poetry, *Scratching Lottery Tickets on a Street Corner*, was published in 2018 by Finishing Line Press.

Sue Buck has lived in the North Quabbin area her entire life. Although she has always loved writing, Sue had never had her work published until now. It has been a thrill for her to participate in the publication of Mountains and Meditations. She finds writing to be a wonderful compulsion and hopes that she never loses that spark. Sue believes she inherited her love of writing from her mother, and hopes to pass it along to her children and grandchildren.

Nancy Damon Burke grew up in Greenfield, Massachusetts, near Highland Pond. Teeming with frogs and aquatic life her love of nature probably began there. She has written stories for all ages. A champion of dogs, Nancy prefers their company to most people, writing daily alongside her trusty companion, Nelson.

Kathy Chencharik is a freelance writer whose poetry, non-fiction, and fiction have appeared in several newspapers, magazines, and anthologies including, *A Patchwork Christmas, Thin Ice* a 2010 Level Best Books: Crime stories by New England Writers, where her story *The Book Signing* won the 2011 Derringer Award for Best Flash Story, *Uniquely North Quabbin* by Haley's, *Time's Reservoir* by Quabbin Quills, *Blunt Flash Trauma* by Randall Dewitt, and the newest, *Flash in the Can: Number One*, which include eight honorable mentions she received in Alfred Hitchcock Mystery Magazine for their "Mysterious Photograph contest".

Liz Day enjoys running and hiking through the woods. She runs many trail and other types of races such as; triathlons, Obstacle Course races, team relays, including a 31-mile mountain Ultra Marathon at Wachusett Mountain last summer. The long hours of training in the woods alone with her trusty dog, Gator Girl, is therapeutic, primal, and meditation in motion. She hopes she inspires others to get off the couch and get into nature.

Kay Deans lives on a small farm in north central Massachusetts with her husband Peter, her German shepherd dog Lady and an eclectic collection of goats, sheep and guardian animals. Also an occasional cow and pony. She was the founding editor of *CryoGas International* and has more than 40 feature articles published in *New England Country Folks* and *Country Folks Grower.*

Childhood found **Ned Green** enjoying and exploring the woods of Wendell and Warwick with his friends. Old stone foundations were dug through to find assorted treasures such as old blue bottles. His passion for the woods captivated him his whole life of 26 years. He graduated from the College of the Atlantic in Bar Harbor, Maine where he simply wrote in his college yearbook, "I Worship Mountains!"

He told his Ma, "I've hiked every trail there is here in Maine. Next I need to go the White Mountains of New Hampshire." He did. He subsequently worked for all the New England Mountain Clubs as

Caretaker and Trail Maintainer until an ice climbing accident in 2001 claimed his life. A scholarship is awarded in his name each year to a Pioneer Valley Regional (PVRSD) graduating senior.

A fundraising hike is offered each year to hike Mt. Grace in Warwick, 10:00 to noon, always the Saturday of Mother's Day weekend. All are welcome!

Visit **Ned-Green.com** for more information.

Sharon A. Harmon is a freelance writer and poet. She writes for the Uniquely Quabbin Magazine. She has two chapbooks of poetry Swimming with Cats and Wishbone in a Lightning Jar. Sharon is featured in a new book Flash in the Can Number One, with two flash mysteries and is currently working on a story for Flash in the Can Number Two. You can find her at Facebook at "Sharon A. Harmon writer and poet," and at Sharon Ann Harmon Publishing.

Dennis F. King started writing short stories three years ago. He enjoys recalling memories of his life experiences. A top computer tech for the Raytheon Co., now retired, has three sons and three grandchildren he adores. It is his opinion that writing is as easy as talking.

Karyl J. Leslie has been an ordained minister in the United Church of Christ since 1986. She served parishes in Pennsylvania, Massachusetts and Indiana. She is now retired and living in her home state of Massachusetts. In addition to pastoral ministry, she worked for several years in the mental health field. Previously published books include *Rays of Hope: Poems of Faith and Inspiration* (2014) and *Sparkling Light: Poems of Wonder and Grace* (2016), both published by Xlibris and available online at Amazon, Barnes and Noble, and Xlibris.com.

Joanne McIntosh has lived in Chelmsford most of her life and moved to Athol four years ago. She attended Mt. Wachusett Community College and Fitchburg State University, and after graduation, taught the sixth grade in Ayer. Joanne is now a Life Coach for Kids and an author of children's books. She is an active member of the Montachusett Suicide Prevention Task Force, the Heywood Healthcare Charitable Foundation, Quabbin Writers, the Berkshire Women Writers Group in Stockbridge, and the Society of Children's Book Writers and Illustrators. Joanne has a grown daughter and a teenage granddaughter who live in Grafton. Simba, a 35-pound Maine Coon cat, lives with her, and they both love exploring new exciting places in the North Quabbin.

Steven Michaels is the author of *Sweet Life of Mystery*, a parody of the whodunit genre. He has been featured on *The Satirist* website for his scintillating take on current affairs, and has written and produced over twenty plays for students as school director for the Drama Club. Steve founded the Quabbin Quills in 2017 and was instrumental in creating the first anthology, *Time's Reservoir*. He is so thankful to all the authors who have come to share his writer's dream.

Mary Owen's life has been a journey of light. She has worked as a counselor in women's shelters and homeless shelters in the Detroit area. In 2008 she answered the call to become an ordained Elder in the United Methodist Church and now pastors a church congregation in Athol, Massachusetts. In her quest for the truth of her beginnings, she is currently researching her heritage. She has two adult children and five grandchildren. Mary's life mission is to sow seeds of God's hope and love, to bring light into a dark world.

Maggie Scarf is the author of six books for adults, including the acclaimed *New York Times* bestsellers *Unfinished Business: Pressure Points in the Lives of Women* and *Intimate Partners: Patterns in Love and Marriage*. She is also the author of two books for children. She has appeared on many television programs, including *Oprah, Today Show, Good Morning America, CBS News,* and *CNN*. She currently blogs for *Psychology Today*.

Sally Sennott is a graduate of Duke University. She was a long-time resident of Athol and recently moved to southern New Hampshire.

She is a retired newspaper correspondent and editor of a local museum newsletter. Sally has written two plays as well as a children's story that were produced into videos and featured on the Athol cable access channel (AOTV).

Nancy Tatro is a lifelong resident of Athol. As a novice writer, this is her first published work. She is a member of the Quabbin Writers Group and participates in two book clubs at the Athol Public Library.

Jan VanVaerenewyck has been sitting by her pond for 15 years. She shares the view with her chickens, ponies, cats, dog and husband. When not jotting down poems, essays and stories she is quilting, knitting and gardening. Jan's poems have appeared in *Taproot* and *The Aurorean*. She is a member of the Louise Bogan Poets of Lunenberg and has been published in their recent anthology *Sudden Marigold*.

Sonya Wirtanen lives in Phillipston, Massachusetts and has loved writing ever since she learned to rhyme. It was not until recently that she began taking her passion more seriously. Her inspiration comes from her experience as an educator, a foster parent, a yoga teacher and most recently, as an AmeriCorps volunteer. Sonya finds that writing teaches her to live more mindfully by reflecting on the places she has been and the people she meets, taking time to slow down and enjoy the present moment.

Made in the USA
Middletown, DE
12 May 2019